RAPTOR CANYON

A.W. Baldwin

© 2018 A.W. Baldwin
All Rights Reserved

This is a work of fiction. The characters, incidents, and dialogues are products of the author's imagination and are not to be construed as real. Any resemblance to actual events or persons, living or dead, is entirely coincidental.

Copyright 2018 by A. W. Baldwin

ISBN	978-0-9996913-2-8	Hardbound
ISBN	978-0-9996913-3-5	Paperback
ISBN	978-0-9996913-5-9	ebook

All rights reserved. No part of this book may be used or reproduced in any manner without the written permission of the author, except in the case of brief quotations embodied in critical articles or reviews.

Cover art by Nate Baldwin.

An impromptu murder leads a hermit named Relic to an unlikely set of dinosaur petroglyphs and swindlers using the unique rock art to turn a pristine canyon into a high-end tourist trap. When attorney, Wyatt, and his boss travel to the site to approve the next phase of financing, Wyatt learns the truth about their unorthodox role in the project. A corrupt security chief runs Relic and Wyatt off of the site and the unusual pair must endure each other while fleeing though white-water rapids, remote gorges, and hidden caverns. Faye, who shares covert ties with the treasured site, catalyzes their desperate plan to fight back and to recast the fate of Raptor Canyon.

A Five Star Rating from Reader's Favorites

"Raptor Canyon is a hoot of an adventure novel, and it's most highly recommended."

"A terrific book... a fast-moving tale..."

"Fantastic descriptions of the majestic canyons and tense action sequences keep you anxiously turning the pages..."

"...well-defined characters move this exciting story along with plenty of surprises and scares."

"Well done... action packed."

"Baldwin's writing style fits the action-oriented story to a tee, making it easy to visualize the rugged canyon country and natural settings."

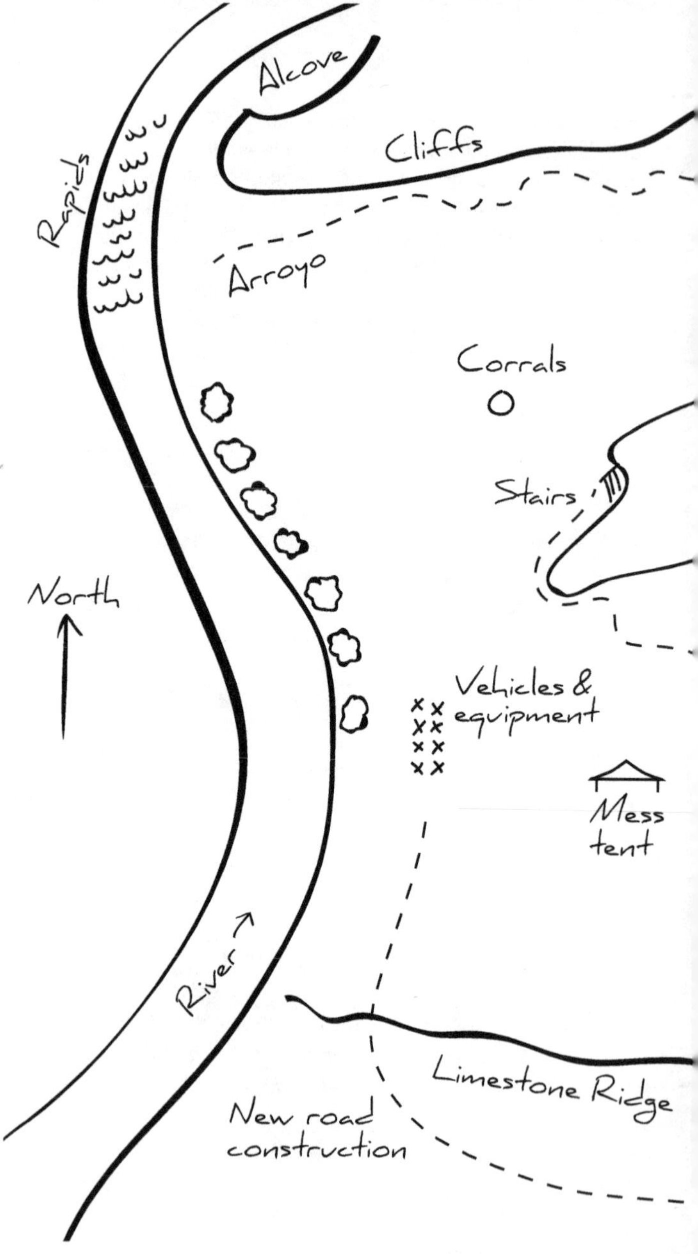

Alcove
Cliffs
Rapids
Arroyo
Corrals
Stairs
North
Vehicles &
equipment
Mess
tent
River
Limestone Ridge
New road
construction

Limestone Hills

Cave

Cliffs

✕ Petroglyphs

Tents

Horse
trail

Road

. . . .

Chapter 1

He took a wooden match from its box, set the red sulfur tip against the molar by his canine, and pulled it from his mouth with a hard twist. The match exploded into flame just beyond his lips. He turned the propane burner full-on, and the familiar metallic sneeze flared, then settled into a steady burn.

Most folks in the high country called him Old Man Snow, eighty-nine years and counting, with full, riotous hair the color of his name, and caramel eyes that squeezed into narrow slits when he laughed. Snow had herded Red Angus cattle over six hundred acres and trained his own quarter horses for seven decades. He'd explored deep into the canyons along the powerful Green and Colorado rivers, hunting rabbits, coyotes, mountain sheep and deer. A cornered puma nearly tore out his throat in Four Mile Canyon the year he turned twenty-one, but he'd shot the clever cat at the last second. He knew nearly every trail, cliff face, and ancient pueblo ruin on his family ranch.

He set the tea kettle on top and turned back toward the kitchen counter.

Cancer had taken Snow's wife when she was only fifty years old. Six years later, his son and daughter in law died together at the hands of a drunk driver in Heber City. After that, his grand-daughters moved to the ranch and he raised them all by himself, the best way he knew how. Smart and tough, they'd learned to ride, hay, irrigate, and operate all manner of tractor, bailer, and roller mill. One was now a freshman at the University at Salt Lake, one a senior in business administration at Laramie, Wyoming. He would do whatever it took to help them succeed, but he needed cash. World economics had reached the Utah backcoun-try and depressed cattle prices beyond what he could bear.

He pulled the old fish-gutting knife from the drawer and fiddled with the split wooden handle, pushing the duct tape that circled it back into place. Where did he put the bread?

He'd called their family lawyer, Bob Bartlett, a friendly, old-school counsellor who'd retired years ago. Bartlett explained that he had sold his small firm to a group of lawyers in Denver who spe-cialized in representing ranchers and farmers. An attorney in the big firm had proposed a solution for Old Man Snow, one he did not relish but could not afford to ignore.

He looked at the clock on the kitchen wall. Was the lawyer coming today, or tomorrow?

He stared at random nicks in the countertop,

then looked up at slices of bread on a plate by the refrigerator. For a turkey sandwich, wasn't it? His mind wandered to a memory of a beautiful roan he'd bought as a colt down in Flagstaff. One of his favorite horses, smart and spirited.

A loud rap on the door jarred him. He pushed away from the counter, turned, and walked to the front door of the old farmhouse, the sound of his cowboy boots clunking on the hard pine floor.

"Mr. Snow?" A man with a henna brown, close-cropped beard stood at the door. His teeth, Hollywood white, cut a humorless swath through the tight curls and his eyes shone like beetles. He wore a dark blue, pin-stripe suit with creases that could slice paper. A stylish red tie knotted tightly against his windpipe. He carried a hard-sided briefcase in his left hand.

"Come in out of the sun," Snow said, opening the screen door, offering his palm.

The man pumped Snow's hand like a congressman.

"That I will, Mr. Snow. It's starting to really heat up."

"No air conditioning down here, just a little unit up in the bedroom," Snow said, turning and motioning the lawyer into the living room. "Have a seat."

The lawyer sat on the edge of the couch, its floral pattern worn off the cushions in places. Snow noticed the man scan the spacious room, his eyes following the wooden trim along the floor and around the doorways to a cherry wood dresser across from the couch and, next to it, a waist-high bookcase. The lawyer glanced at a tall mirror by the door to the kitchen where a marble top table collected all manner of loose magazines, envelopes, and bills. He set his briefcase on the coffee table and popped open the latches.

"Have you thought of any other questions or concerns about this transaction?" the lawyer asked.

"Would you like a turkey sandwich?"

"No, but thanks," the lawyer said.

"What transaction?" Snow asked.

"You know," the lawyer said slowly, "the one we've been discussing on the phone. The new company that will hold Little Horse Canyon, on the far edge of your ranch, and give you the cash you need for your granddaughters…" The attorney began pulling documents from his briefcase and laying them on the table.

Snow felt the answer near at hand, but just out of reach. "Remind me," he said.

"The deal you and Mr. Bartlett discussed. We have formed a limited liability company called Little Horse Canyon, L.L.C. You will own half the shares, half the assets – the canyon itself – and the investors will hold the other shares."

"I'll own half?"

"Yes, just as we've been discussing."

"And my granddaughters get my share when I die?"

"Of course."

Snow gazed through the window at the grassy hill beyond. "Bob Bartlett set all this up, right?" The idea began to feel more familiar to him.

"That's right, Bob got us all set up. All we need to do today is sign this paperwork."

"Oh, sure, Bob. Me and him caught his first catfish in Little Horse Canyon." Snow gazed into the distant memory, displayed in his mind like a grainy video. "Took a hammer to the thing to finally kill it, you know. Hard to kill those things, but they're good eatin'." He looked back at the lawyer. "Great guy."

"You bet, a great guy. Here's the company agreement. You need to sign here." The lawyer pointed to the page.

"You've got to see something first, from above Little Horse Canyon, something Bob thought was really neat, the cat's meow." Snow went to the waist-high bookshelf and touched a slab of rock that lay on top. "Over here," he motioned.

The lawyer released a slow sigh, stood, and walked to the rough-cut stone. His expression seemed a little pained until he saw the fossil Snow was pointing to. His mouth opened in surprise as he examined the outline of a fossilized dinosaur jaw with bone-slicing fangs.

"This is the real thing, isn't it?" he asked, running a finger along the mandible.

"Sure is. Found it a few miles north, up above Little Horse Canyon, already loose from the other stones up there. I think there's big dinosaur fossils all through that layer of rock nobody's found yet."

"Impressive," the lawyer said, rubbing the edge of the rock. "You found this in Little Horse Canyon?"

"About five miles away."

"Oh."

"Out past the ruins and the rock art."

"Rock art?"

"What?" Snow suddenly remembered a pledge he'd made to a friend, a promise not to reveal a remote set of petroglyphs they'd found there. He felt like he'd said too much.

"Petroglyphs in the canyon?"

"Hell, I can't remember now. Maybe. Maybe not. Might be remembering Horse Creek Canyon, a whole other place," Snow chuckled nervously. He looked at the fossil and patted the stone.

"Well, should we get back to the business at hand?" the lawyer asked. "The sale that Bob set up for you?"

"Bob did this?"

"Well, he got us together, and we took it from there, but, yes, Bob was involved."

"I helped Bob catch his first catfish, right there in Little Horse Canyon."

"Yes."

Snow shuffled back to the coffee table and sat on the couch. He thumbed through the thirty-page document.

"Look all right to you?" the lawyer asked.

"Sure," Snow said, though part of him was not sure at all. "This is what Bob said to do…"

"Yes. Here's a pen. We need to sign the agreement, the warranty deed, the shares transfer and several disclosures and disclaimers, all in order and ready to go."

Snow hesitated.

"Then, I can deliver the check to you for

$150,000. The money for your granddaughters to finish school and to keep your ranch going another year."

The money. Snow felt his stomach start to clench. He desperately needed money for the girls, for their tuition, rent, food. And to run the ranch, buy the cattle feed, pay the veterinarian, replace the clutch on the tractor. He knew he could trust Bob to set all this up.

Snow watched the lawyer stare at the fossil for a moment, something lighting his eyes, making the corners of his mouth rise up a tiny bit. Snow knew the spark of an idea when it flashed in a man's head. He wondered for a moment what the attorney was thinking about, then remembered he was hungry for lunch. Damn. Was that a turkey sandwich he was making?

The tea kettle began to whistle.

"Hand me the pen," said Snow.

Chapter 2

Two Years Later

A morning breeze tickled through his thin goatee, black and shiny as a crow's wing. Relic had been holed up at one of his stills, a few miles north, tucked under a deep sandstone ledge. A nice spot for cooking gin. At high water every spring, a thin drizzle rained from a hundred feet above his shelter, and fresh driftwood for his fire collected by the river's edge. He'd been exploring a gorge above the still when he saw a column of smoke reaching into the early sky. He'd gathered his pack and hiked miles upriver to see what kind of men disturbed this remote canyon.

Descended from unlikely ancestors of the Hopi and Scottish Tribes, some thought him a wandering recluse, a trespasser, a moonshiner. Others saw a monk of the ghost-filled pueblos, a relic at home in the ruins, gorges, and desert canyons.

He held the binoculars to his eyes.

Three men were hiking away from their camp, coming along a well-worn trail toward Relic. He lowered himself to the ground. The path made a sharp turn where he knelt, hugging a ridge that pointed back toward the flatter, open part of the canyon. These men were likely to stay on the trail, so he kept himself low and moved past the bend, toward where they were heading. Once out of their line of sight, he stood and trotted down the wide path. He knew from visits here years ago that it led east along the ridge until it reached a high, sheer cliff, where it turned north again and eventually led to another gorge within the larger canyon.

He watched the ground as he ran until he came to the foot of the sandstone cliff. Something unfamiliar filled his periphery. He stopped. Relic squinted at a newly built set of wooden stairs, the pine still straw-colored and shiny in the desert sun.

"What the…?"

He shifted the weight of his pack and looked up. Four-by-four posts, reinforced with criss-crossed two-by-fours, rose upward toward the top of the cliff. Slatted stairs were nailed to the under frame and railings guarded their way to the top. The steps switched back twice before the stiff frame ended above the sheer rock face.

Those stairs belong at some public park, he mused, some Sunday afternoon boardwalk, with hotdog stands, ice cream, kids clutching helium balloons on strings. Deep in the maze of neck-craning cliffs and naked hoodoos, out among the coyotes, cougars, and rattlers, well, Relic thought, they were like tits on a catfish. Way the hell out of place.

He calculated how far the men were behind him.

He tightened the straps on his pack and ran up the stairs, balancing on the railing as he went. He would have to be quick or the men would see him out here in the open. He worked to keep his breaths deep and regular, pulling in his air when his right foot was up, expelling it when his right foot was down. He moved past the short platform at the first switchback and kept going, concentrating on each stair. At the second switchback, he turned briefly to check the trail below. Empty. The men had not yet rounded the corner.

He put his head down and pushed hard through the final rise of stairs. At the top, he found a trail between the brush and boxelder saplings and ducked into them. He rested with his hands on his knees and pulled air into his lungs until his head cleared and he could slow his breath. Cautiously, he peered beyond the edge of the cliff.

Three men appeared down below as they rounded the side of the ridge and made their way toward the staircase. Relic moved back from the cliff and trotted along the trail on even ground. He remembered this place from a long time ago, when he'd come here with a friend. But without the man-made stairs, the cliff could be scaled only by experienced climbers with ropes. Relic and his friend had come from the other direction, a hazardous trek over car-sized boulders and two-story crags.

He walked farther along the winding path

and reached an open area at the base of another cliff that reached about a hundred feet above the floor. The sandstone was smooth in most places, coated with a thin layer of minerals deposited over thousands of years. He searched the cliff up and down, moving parallel with the bluff and into the center of the open area. He wasn't sure just exactly where he was on this little plateau.

Voices startled him, suddenly sharp and clear, level with the ridge where he stood. He ran quickly past the open area to a jumble of rocks and made his way through them. The men were close now, their throated sounds dividing now and then into recognizable words. Relic pulled himself up to a high piece of sandstone and found a place to rest just below its rim. He removed his pack and peered between the rocks, toward the clearing below.

One man, tall and rail-thin, stopped and waited for the other two. A younger man with curly blond hair was talking excitedly, explaining something about hard work and talent. A shorter man, built like a weight lifter, followed the blond to the center of the open area.

There, the blond moved to the cliff face and carefully pulled something away from the rock. Relic heard the rip of peeling tape and watched as the blond man rolled a small plastic tarp into a ball and tossed it aside. The other men moaned in admiration and moved closely to examine the stone. The blond crossed his arms in self-satisfaction and swaggered behind them.

The muscle man adjusted his hat and stepped away from the cliff and behind the blond. The tall man worked his way down the rock face, back toward the trail, examining as he went.

"Won't pay the rent," he heard the blond man say. "Travel plans."

The muscle man turned toward the blond. "Hell…" he said. He began cursing the blond, who uncrossed his arms and backed away.

The tall man turned toward the other two.

Muscle man reached under his shirt.

The blond raised his hands to his face, a useless reflex.

A shot cracked through the canyon like the pierce of lightening, jarring Relic's teeth, snapping his bones to attention. The shock echoed against the high cliffs in overlapping waves, then grew fainter and fainter, leaving a void as profound as the emptiness of outer space.

. . . .

Chapter 3

Relic realized he'd seen it all happen, just now, in the living breath of an instant in time, when muscle man pulled his dark pistol, the blond's head jerked forward and back, and he folded and fell to the ground so fast Relic's mind could not register the surreal event until after it had happened.

Blond man lay motionless in the dirt. Particles of dust suspended in the air above him. Muscle man stood there like a statue. Then, he turned slowly and put his pistol into a side holster beneath his shirt. Tall man trotted toward him, his arms wide.

"What the hell?"

"…more…"

"Warn me next time…"

"Had to anyway…that."

"Yeah, but now…"

Muscle man waved his hands downward as he spoke, assuring the tall man.

Tall man raised his hands in mock surrender

and turned on his heel. He spun back and complained "…always the hard way with you."

A lone crow called across the expanse. The two men stopped talking and began to scan the area, looking along the trail and then back toward the field of rocks where Relic hid. He moved his head slightly downward, keeping the men in his periphery, not wanting them to recognize a pair of eyes among the boulders.

Tall man looked back to his companion and seemed to take charge. "Now we have to go back and get a stretcher…" He pointed at the blond on the ground.

Muscle man shrugged.

"Get somebody else to help you."

"You can be a little bitch, sometimes."

"We could've worked it out with the guy…" Tall man spread his arms and began to walk away.

Muscle man glanced around quickly and then followed his companion down the trail.

Relic took a deep breath. What had seemed interminable had happened in only a few moments. Quietly, he lifted his pack onto his shoulders and looked back to the blond. The man's arm twitched ever so slightly, and the movement, so sudden, so spectral, sent an electric jolt up Relic's spine.

"Shit-damn." He clenched his teeth.

The two men disappeared around a bend in the path, but Relic could still hear their ghostly sounds, boots scraping the hard ground, syllables echoing through the air.

Relic moved carefully down from his perch.

He circled opposite the cliff and the blond man,
a mix of raw nerves and superstition shying him
away. He could still hear the other men as they
wound through the tall brush and toward the
wooden staircase.

Relic took a breath and ran to the fallen man.
The blond's face was sideways in the sandy soil and
a fine layer of dust had settled on his clothes. His
right arm was flung to his side. Relic kneeled and
felt the man's wrist for a pulse. He found one.

Relic slid his pack to the ground then gently
turned the man onto his back. The blond's eyes
were closed, his reddened cheek coated in sand.
Relic brushed his eyelids and face and carefully
rested the man's head onto the pack. The man
seemed almost peaceful, in a sleepy sort of way,
until Relic straightened his legs and then the man's
eyes tightened in pain and he let loose a low, rum-
bling moan.

Relic cupped his hand over the man's mouth
and stared down the trail, listening for any change
in the sounds from the other men.

"Shh, stay quiet."

The blond took a short breath and seemed to
pass out again. Relic pulled his water bottle from
a side pocket on his pack and set it next to them,
ready to offer a drink. The man's chin was narrow,
effeminate. Relic moved it slowly back and forth,
trying to rouse him a bit, make sure he stayed alive.

Blood soaked the front of the man's shirt, its
iron-sulfur smell throwing Relic back to another
time, another life, when he'd lost a friend to rifle
fire, a man who'd stood right beside him the mo-

ment before, a whole, live person with family and a purpose and a life to imagine ahead of him. One second was all it took. Relic shook his head and tried to clear it.

The blond began to mutter to himself, not fully aware of Relic, not quite conscious enough to know what had happened. Relic held his breath.

"What?" The blond's eyes snapped open and his voice carried across the clearing.

Relic clamped his hand over the man's mouth. "Shush, man, the guys who shot you are close."

"Oh, god," he said quietly.

"Why did they shoot you?"

The man took a shallow breath and his lips began to twitch. His eyelids flittered and closed.

"Hang on."

"Hoax," the blond whispered, swinging his head back and forth.

"Take it easy, man," Relic said, bracing the man's head against the pack. "I'll go get help."

"No, no…" the blond said again, "there's treasure there, real deal, look…" The man lapsed into silence. His lips drooped. His eyes, thankfully, never opened again, the tension in his muscles slackened and he slid off the pack and fully onto the ground. Relic felt the man's neck for a beat and found none. Though a stranger, Relic felt the loss of this man too.

"Damn it to hell." Relic's lungs squeezed the air out in a rush and his muscles froze in place. His brain felt suddenly cold and rigid, his soul immobile. He stared into the dust at his knees and slowly felt for his own memory of this place, just

beyond him, somewhere in the dusk. He sensed
a deep throb of the canyon, broader than just one
man, and he felt the cool of the sand, the brush
of the breeze, an impression of all the people who
must have lived and died here over the centuries
and only after what felt like a very long time he
began to feel the warmth return to his hands and
the pump of blood in his ears, and he turned fully
away from the blond man's lifeless chest.

The blond's shoes were crusted in red dirt,
holes frayed just behind the small toe of each foot.
His jeans were wrapped at the waist with a tool belt
of sorts, a ballpeen hammer twisted on its strap, a
pair of chisels spilled out onto the dirt.

Relic dragged his pack away from the man's
head. He hoisted the pack onto his back and
grabbed his water bottle from the ground. Keeping
his eyes away from the dead man's face, he shuffled
toward the nearby wall, to the spot the three men
had pointed to a short time ago. He moved closer
to a panel of flat, chocolate-colored cliff that rose
twenty feet from the sandy soil.

There, etched into the sandstone, stood two
petroglyph warriors stationed by an array of liz-
ard-shaped forms and alligator heads. In the midst
of them was the yawning jaw and naked skull of a
flesh-eating dinosaur.

Chapter 4

"Wyatt!" Todd William Winford, IV, filled the doorway, blocking the hallway light behind him.

Wyatt sat ram-rod straight, his daydream scraped away like a metal fork dragged across a dinner plate.

"Yes, sir?" Documents were stacked around Wyatt's desk like a paper fortress. He strained his neck to see above them.

Winford gave a quick sneer at the mess. "What's all this?"

"Getting deposition exhibits and questions lined up for Mr. Reed." Wyatt straightened his tie. "I was looking for Exhibit 135E."

"Well, get it done by tonight. Something's come up and I need your assistance."

"Sure, Mr. Winford."

In his early fifty's, Winford wore his graying brown hair short against his head and sported a tight beard. He favored three-piece suits with dark, crisp vests. His eyes were all business, no mirth, his

skin a starchy pale. Winford was a senior partner
at Reed, Rosen, and Hoyle, one of the largest law
firms in Denver. Their practice spanned five states
and focused on real property litigation, estate planning, corporate work, and business deals.

"And turn some more light on." Winford
flipped the switch on Wyatt's desk lamp. "It's dark
as a witch's cave in here."

"Wait...tonight?" Wyatt asked. "I've got to
read and draft questions for all those exhibits." He
pointed to two stacks of papers on the floor.

"We've got a field trip to Utah tomorrow.
The jet leaves the tarmac at eight in the morning,
sharp."

"All right, I'll figure it out." It was only
mid-morning. He could get maybe half of his work
done by supper and then pull an all-nighter.

"Bring some hiking boots. For a change, this
will not be our usual business meeting."

"Sure. May I ask: is James going with us?"
James Cross was Winford's lead associate. Wyatt
was one of several newer associates and worked for
all of the more senior attorneys.

"I had hoped he could come," Winford
glanced at his fingernails, "but he's home with the
flu. You'll do."

"How long will we be gone?"

"One night, two at the most. No need for suit
and tie. In fact, we'll be in a four-wheel drive from
the airport to the development site. We'll meet the
owner, who wants us to see the scope of the project
and work through some of his concerns."

"Well," Wyatt scanned his desktop. "Might be

fun to get out into the fresh air."

"It'll be a pain in the ass. Bring your laptop fully charged. No electricity out there yet." Winford turned and disappeared through the door.

"Well," Wyatt mumbled to himself, "better order some pizza for lunch. And supper." If he kept going into the early morning tomorrow, he could run home to change clothes and pack and then get some sleep on the flight. What kind of business deal would get Todd William Winford, IV, to a remote spot in the Utah outback?

James, Winford's right hand man, was out sick. This could be a real opportunity, Wyatt thought. Winford was haughty, sure enough, but he was a brilliant attorney and he'd gained a reputation as a tough business negotiator. If Wyatt did a stand-up job, he'd get noticed, maybe work again with Winford, maybe become part of the mid-level team instead of bottom man on the ladder. This could be the start of something great.

Wyatt tried again to focus on Exhibit 135E and what Mr. Reed ought to ask the witness at his deposition.

. . . .

Chapter 5

Relic climbed through the boulder field above and east of the petroglyphs, re-living the feel of the blond man's pulse, the scratch of his voice, his final collapse. Anger fueled the churning of his legs and the pump of his heart as he rose to the top of the pile of rocks.

"Sonofabitch." He clenched his fist. He was going to find out what these bastards were doing here in this remote canyon. And put a stop to it.

The ground leveled out in front of him, and he could see a way to cross over to the other narrow plateau to the south. The two ridges ran roughly parallel to each other. As far as he could tell, the only way to the canyon floor was either back from where he'd come and down those wooden stairs or to the southern ridge and downslope from there. The longer route would take him all day, but he didn't like the exposure he'd risked earlier, coming up the staircase.

He worked his way to the south until he was

in the middle of the other ridge then turned west,
toward the main canyon. There was no trail here,
but the ground was open.

What did the blond man mean when he said
"treasure," he wondered. Why had the muscle man
killed him? Had the blond pulled a "hoax" on the
other two men? Or they on him?

He eventually crossed a bench that dropped
him to a lower elevation and then came to an
area of rolling ground with scattered cactus and
juniper. By then, the sun had begun its arc toward
evening. He figured he was above and a bit south
of the man-camp that tall man, muscle man, and
the blond had left this morning. There ought to be
a good look-out spot on the edge of the plateau. He
continued west for another half-mile then stopped
for a long drink of water.

A deep, metallic snort rode on the canyon
breeze. He turned and trotted toward the sound,
weaving around scrub pine and prickly pear until
he crested a small rise. He leaned against a couch-
sized rock and put the binoculars to his eyes.

Downslope, the terrain spread and flattened
before reaching a rugged limestone ridge. To the
left of the low ridge, a yellow monster snorted
again and seemed to paw at the earth, its blade
rising and falling to the ground. The dozer turned
and aimed its heavy armor, then plowed its nose
into the dirt. Ribbons of soil and sage sheared from
the surface and rolled aside as the machine carved
a meandering game trail into a straight, flat line.
Something the family minivan could drive across.

"What jackass is leading this mule train?"

Relic asked himself. He ran his fingers through his goatee and peered through the binoculars again.

Two rusted pickup trucks sat near a backhoe on the edge of the new road. One man sat on the end of a tailgate, moving something in his hands.

A high-pitched whine grew louder and louder as something buzzed through the air, winding its way up the hill. It was coming right at him. The man on the rear of the truck watched the thing as it rose quickly along the slope. The man looked familiar. Muscle man, he realized – the one who'd shot the blond at the petroglyphs.

Relic spun from the rock and ran across the broken ground as quickly as he could. Past a low pine tree, around a large rock, along the edge of prickly pear, he sped back across the ridge. It sounded like a miniature chainsaw dogging him, closing in. He ran to the edge of a steep wash and slid down the slope, working his boots across the sand like skis on powdered snow. At the bottom, he moved behind a lone fin of sandstone and tossed his pack on the ground.

The drone seemed to lose him for a moment, its sound becoming distant. He rummaged through his pack, wrapped his fingers on the Colt special, and pulled it out. He'd loaded it with special shells so it fired like a shotgun, sending a spread of tiny shot at his target instead of a single bullet. The special ammunition was better for dealing with snakes, when he had to.

The sound seemed to be circling him. Of course, he realized – it had a camera. The muscle man on the pickup truck could see Relic, could raise the drone in the air until it found him, then zoom in closer.

He shouldered the pack again and ran along a shallow arroyo. The sound of the aircraft changed again as it banked sharply and bore down on him. There was no way to outrun it. Relic slid to his knees behind a low rock, slid off the pack, and raised his pistol. The drone kept coming at him, as if to ram straight into his face. He aimed and fired, the blast muffled by the walls of the dry gulch.

The drone sputtered and sparked, then fell, dead weight, to the ground. Relic hurried to the machine and scooped a hole in the sand with his boots. He pushed the drone into the shallow bowl and jumped up and down on it, smashing its pieces as flat as he could. "Damn you to hell!" he shouted, almost as nervous as he was angry. He covered it with sand and laid a flat piece of stone on top.

Not perfect, but maybe the muscle man would lose time searching for the thing.

Relic zipped his pistol into an outer pocket on his pack, shouldered it again, and trotted farther up the arroyo, away from the dead drone and anyone looking for it.

Chapter 6

A milky haze brushed the blue horizon like watercolor paint. Burnt sandstone cliffs stood resolutely beneath the sky. Below the rock wall, a row of cottonwoods twisted along the unseen river but Schmidt could hear the low grumble of water a mile away, spring run-off filling the swollen channel with the ash and mud of countless mountain creeks. Low sagebrush and grasses grew on the gentle upslope where he stood. Not yet noon, the temperature was already in the mid-eighties.

He wiped his nose with a faded yellow handkerchief and took a breath. Standing just over six-foot-two, his lanky frame made him seem even taller. His lips pressed thin against themselves, ever taut. He removed his dark sunglasses. His eyes were pale blue, round, with thin sacks, like melted wax, pooled underneath. He surveyed the area. Schmidt was not a talkative man by nature, but, by god, this project was going to be a cash cow, a business venture finally come to completion that would send him into early, high-roller, retirement, and he had trouble keeping quiet about it sometimes.

But he was going to have to keep Lynch, his impulsive chief of security, under control. Schmidt had let Lynch make all the arrangements with the artist, but shooting him up there, right at the petroglyph site, was unsettling. Schmidt hadn't expected that and had refused to help move the blond man's body. Lynch was going to have to take care of that part of the arrangement too.

About a hundred yards away, cream-colored canvas flapped in the breeze as workers finished anchoring a large mess tent to a wooden floor. Schmidt spotted Lynch walking away from the giant canopy. Schmidt put his glasses back on and waved him over.

"Have you got the new coolers hooked up yet?" Schmidt asked.

"Just about," he replied. Lynch's forehead was broad, his chin narrow. His frosted eyes peered at Schmidt with an unnatural intensity, tiny lights cranked too high. A former army weapons sergeant, dishonorably discharged, Lynch was now a private security consultant. The project needed a good security man and someone to hire and keep the workers in line. Barrel-chested and muscled like a weight lifter, Lynch could crack the whip on the toughest of crews. And he shared Schmidt's view about how to get things done under budget too. Schmidt had to pay for the surveyors and engineers up front. But the workers here to dig the trenches, erect the sheds and corrals, cook for the crew, and work the heavy equipment – Lynch paid them in cash, off the books. Lynch knew just how to do it, who to hire, who to avoid. Lynch had five percent of the action, the right kind of motivation for success. Though lop-sided, it made them – plus one other man – partners in this business venture.

"The blond guy. The body, I mean. Taken care of?" Schmidt asked.

"Thought you didn't want to know," Lynch said.

Schmidt stared at Lynch from behind his sunglasses.

"Yes." Lynch finally nodded. "Remember Matt Button? The kick boxer?"

"Sure."

"Button and I took care of it. Just finished up. The body is far and away from here. Only the coyotes will find him."

Schmidt grunted an approval.

"But we may have a problem employee on our hands."

"Oh?"

"Yesterday, I was testing out one of our surveillance drones. I saw someone up above the patch of limestone, where the road will cross. I sent up the drone to check it out, and the guy ran from it. When I flew closer, the video died. We went up to look for the drone and it was gone. Don't know if it was a malfunction or if the guy we saw did something to it, but all he had to do was wave at it. Instead, he ran away. That's a guilty conscience, and I don't know what he's feeling guilty about. Not yet, anyway. We're questioning the crew."

"He works for us?" Schmidt asked.

"Don't know who else would be running around this country."

"Probably off drinking when he should be working."

"Yeah, probably. But still…" Lynch watched the workers chop away sagebrush, clearing a path to a row of portable toilets.

"Come up here with me." Schmidt pointed to an outcrop of rock higher up the canyon. They walked together along a small trail to a spot about eighty feet above the encampment and sat.

"We've had to change the route of the main road some. We can see it from here." Schmidt pointed.

Lynch nodded. "That 'S' curve looks different."

"Right. Engineer said we needed to be farther from the river to avoid erosion from spring run-off. But the hotel will still be there, to the right of our mess tent." Schmidt signaled. They'd reviewed the drawings and maps many times, but here, under the piercing sun, cradled between the distant canyon walls, it became three dimensional, real. "The main building, the meeting rooms and gift shop, will still connect through a walkway. We can build each structure separately, on its own schedule. As you know, the water," he pointed behind him, "will come from the spring farther up the canyon. We'll pipe that in for drinking and bottle it for sale too." His grin was tight and straight in the middle, like some part of it was painful.

"Still think we can use some river water?"

"Sure, for irrigation of the grounds, eventually a putting green. And for the horses."

"Still putting a dude ranch over there?" Lynch pointed to makeshift corrals on the north side of the canyon.

"Right near there, yeah. And dudes, for sure, but not much ranch." Schmidt grinned again. "More like horses for tourists to ride up and down river and up parts of the canyon. Trail rides. The final corrals, tack, and supply building will be over there," he pointed to this right. "A nice distance from the hotel, but not too far to walk."

"Good distance for a golf cart ride."

"Right."

"Great setup. Federal land all around us." Lynch pointed his chin to the south.

"Yep. Park and BLM lands," Schmidt said. "We're grand-fathered into a right of way that takes us all the way to the state highway."

"Nice."

Schmidt grunted in agreement.

"Now the road will connect through there?" Lynch asked, pointing high and to their left.

"Yeah, it's not exactly like it looked on our drawings. It will go over that ridge, where the horse trail is now. It's pretty tough limestone there, so we'll need to do some blasting. That's closely regulated, so I'd like to do that right after dark, a couple of days from now."

"It's a helluva spot for tourists." Lynch peered sideways at Schmidt, from under his brow. "When are we gonna show our esteemed partner the special attraction?"

Schmidt's penciled lips curled in what, for

him, passed as a smile.

Chapter 7

Wyatt lingered in the hot shower, steaming the sleepiness from his bones. He dried, shaved, and dressed quickly in nylon cargo pants, running shoes, and one of those sun-block, long sleeve shirts. He used his toothbrush then tossed it in his duffle bag for the overnight trip to Utah. When he realized he'd forgotten to make coffee, he poured yesterday's into a travel cup and microwaved it.

He found the private airport using the map on his phone. When he arrived, he saw a small, white jet on the pavement by the terminal lit with halogen lights, its doorway open, steps hanging toward the ground like a corrugated tongue. He figured it was Winford's plane and hurried on board.

Winford sat in a plush seat across from the door, facing forward. He nodded at Wyatt, who nodded back and greeted the pilot. Winford seemed absorbed in notes on a yellow legal pad, and Wyatt was just as glad not to have to make conversation. In moments, they were airborne. The pilot dimmed the cabin lights and, to the steady hum of the engines, Wyatt fell sound asleep.

Wyatt woke with a bounce as they landed and rolled toward the taxiway. "We're here," he announced.

Winford grunted at the obvious.

Wyatt sipped his cold coffee and slowly re-focused on where he was, wondering what the construction site for the Raptor Canyon project would look like. Was the framing for the main lodge up? Foundations done for the store or the hotel? How many people were working at the site?

They stopped and waited while the engines wound down, their dying whine ringing in his ears. He gathered his duffle and computer bag, took the metal steps to the pavement, and looked around. He heard Winford follow him out of the jet.

The sun was still low on the horizon, a mound of stretched-out honey on distant flats. Winford spoke to the pilot about his and Wyatt's schedule, then they all walked to a low-roofed cinderblock building that served as the private terminal and office. Winford said nothing to Wyatt, so he kept quiet too.

A black, double-cab pickup truck pulled up to the side of the terminal facing the parking lot. Winford nodded toward the truck and Wyatt followed him outside the building. A sun-hardened man named Arnulfo shook their hands and welcomed them. Winford looked at Wyatt and pointed to the front seat.

"Want me to ride shotgun, huh?" Wyatt smiled.

Winford forced a grin and nodded.

Arnulfo put their bags in the rear cab with Winford, and the tires soon sped them over the pavement, tempting Wyatt to doze. After a bit, they turned onto a gravel lane and bounced across the dusty ground until he lost all track of time.

Eventually, they came to a set of wooden corrals and coasted to a stop. The urchin light that rose at the airport had matured into a bright morning sun. Wyatt rolled out of the cab and stretched while Arnulfo strapped his bags to a harness, of sorts, at the rear of a saddle on a sorrel mare.

Wyatt walked cautiously to the reddish-brown horse. Her neck muscles seemed massive, as big at the withers as Wyatt's torso, shifting and bulging under her smooth hide as she swung her head. But her eyes, the size of ripe kiwi, were gentle, feminine. She blinked with lashes the envy of movie stars.

He reached out and patted her shoulder.

Arnulfo motioned for Wyatt to climb onto the sorrel while he tied Winford's bags to the saddle of a gray. Arnulfo helped Winford onto his horse and led him by the bridle. He patted Wyatt's mare on the rump and she moved along the well-worn trail, accustomed to the routine trip, seeking no guidance from the reigns.

They moved across a level path to the edge of a high ridge. Wyatt leaned back in the saddle as his mare started down the rocky trail on the other

side. Sky as clear as spring water spread above
the fertile canyon. Red rock cliffs towered in the
distance. He could see two large drainages that
merged above the gentle slope to the massive river.
The closest arroyo was sharp and deep, rimmed
with rough cliffs and ledges. The farther drainage
seemed to end at a wall of sandstone, an impass-
able box canyon.

Wyatt hadn't ridden a horse since he was
fifteen, when he used to ride with his grandfather,
and he couldn't quite get the feel of it again. He
tried moving loosely with each step of his mare,
counterbalancing as they went, but his rhythm was
off. He turned to look behind him for a moment.

Arnulfo walked along the trail, leading Winford on his speckled gray. Winford rode side-sad-
dle, gripping the saddle horn like the old nag was
going to leap and buck him off at any moment.
Winford's head turned and jarred uncomfortably
with every step of the cautious horse.

Arnulfo had explained that the last part of the
trip was best made by foot or on horseback. A crew
working closer to the river had managed to clear
a rough road for four-wheelers, but the route was
much longer than the horse path and often blocked
by construction.

Sounds of hammering nails, whining engines,
and shovels on dirt reached Wyatt's ears. He
turned toward the noise, back toward the canyon
as it widened before them. Parts of the river were
visible between tall cottonwoods as it snaked its
way from the west. He knew it flowed north here,
at Little Horse Canyon, before it curved back on

itself a dozen miles away, pointed again toward the
Pacific Ocean. A circus-style tent had been raised
on flat ground a short distance from the river. Two
rows of small tents lay roughly parallel to each
other on the east side of the big tent. Men clustered
near a huge square area that had been cleared of
grass and sage, digging what looked like a foun-
dation. Others had carried wood from stacks of
lumber on the southern edge of the small tent city.
Others drove four-wheelers back and forth across
the area, like ants on rubber tires, from the tents
to the shallow square, to a set of wooden sheds,
to a lot filled with pickup trucks, and back again.
The scene reminded him of a Wild West town full
of miners and cowboys and carpenters and bank
robbers.

The trail leveled out and his mare picked up
her pace – she smelled water and hoped to end
her chores for the day. They crossed east of the
giant tent, and Arnulfo shouted to Wyatt to take
the right fork in the trail. This led them to the row
of camps toward the north. At a large canvas tent
near the end of the smaller, camping tents, Arnulfo
stopped, and Wyatt turned his horse around. Winford slid ungracefully from his steed and walked
a few feet away, staying bent at the knees. Wyatt
dismounted and handed the reins to Arnulfo.

"This tent," Arnulfo pointed to a large one
nearby, "is yours, Mister Winford."

"You can bring my bag and briefcase inside."
Winford slowly straightened his legs.

Arnulfo gave a quick roll of his eyes to Wyatt,
who smiled. "You can pick any empty tent you

want," Arnulfo said to Wyatt, nodding toward a row of smaller tents several yards away.

"Thanks." Wyatt began untying his overnight bag and computer case from his mare.

"The really big tent toward the river is the mess hall," Arnulfo said. "Food, water, a place to play cards."

"Sounds good." Wyatt set his bags on the ground and held onto his mare.

"Wyatt, I'm going to take a break for a bit. Be a sport and bring me something to drink and a snack from the mess hall, when you go," Winford said.

"Sure."

Arnulfo shook his head in a quick, subtle move. Winford strode to the front of his tent and disappeared inside. Arnulfo handed Wyatt the reins to Winford's gray. "Be back," he said.

Wyatt rubbed the mare on her forehead and the top of her soft nose. He'd forgotten what teamwork with a good horse felt like, how an entirely separate species of life appreciated a simple pat on the head. Like he did.

When Arnulfo returned, Wyatt handed him the reins to both horses and said: "Thanks again."

"Adios."

Wyatt watched Arnulfo and their horses walk away. He scanned the large, noisy encampment. Smells of manure and diesel fuel mixed in the desert air and it seemed to Wyatt he'd been dropped into another world.

Chapter 8

Arnulfo led the horses to a three-sided shelter and tied one to a post on the left and one on a post to the right. He unstrapped the saddles and lifted the blankets from each and laid them on the ground.

Lynch set out toward the horse shed, making another check of the grounds. He strode directly toward the back of the structure, puzzling about the man he'd chased with the drone, anxious about what he was up to, and how to find him. He rounded the corner quickly, walking straight into the mare Wyatt had ridden. Startled, the horse whinnied in protest and pulled her reigns away from the post. She raised her front hooves then set them lightly to the ground as she backed away, keeping her weight on her haunches, ready to rear again to defend herself.

"Fucking animal!" Lynch raised his hands reflexively and cursed. He put his hand on his holster and glared at the retreating horse.

Arnulfo stepped between them and began to speak to the mare in soothing tones. "Hey, girl, it's OK." He let her smell the back of his hand as he moved slowly toward her. In moments, he had her reigns and began to pet her soft nose.

"What the hell," Lynch said. "Why are these horses here?" His face flushed, he dusted his hands angrily against his pants.

"Just done with a ride from up top," Arnulfo said.

"Well, keep these animals corralled or I'll hire somebody who can."

"Si." Arnulfo walked the mare around Lynch, giving him a wide berth. At the same time, Lynch circled them, keeping his eye on the horse until he was several yards away. Lynch turned and resumed his walk. Arnulfo could hear Lynch cursing him and the mare as he went.

Arnulfo retied the horse to the post and looked up at the sound of boots scraping the ground. A slender, young woman approached from the direction of the mess tent. She carried a bucket of something heavy in each arm, struggling a little under the weight. Her hair was a pretty brunette, her skin tanned mocha. She raised her head as she grew near, and he could see a quick smile, a flash of ivory teeth, a wrinkle of her nose.

"Hola," she said. Water sloshed over the rims as she set the buckets at her feet. "For the horses." She nodded toward the water.

"Gracias." He poured each bucket of water into a metal tub. "You did not have to carry them here by hand." She reminded him of his youngest daughter, Anita. She too had the same confidence, the same broad smile that made you happy to see her.

"I saw you riding in and figured." She shrugged. "Can't let 'em go thirsty for long, not on a day like today." She looked to the glaring sun.

"No." Arnulfo led one horse to drink. "Where do you work? Here?"

"Kitchen."

"Oh, si." He smiled and pointed at her smock.

"You take care of the horses here, don't you? I've seen you working with them."

"Si." He led the first horse back to its post and took the second one to drink.

"Need a hand?"

"You like the horses?"

"Grew up on a ranch." She found a brush hanging from a nail on the inside wall of the shelter. She went to the mare and began to stroke its neck.

"My name is Faye."

"Arnulfo."

"How do you like working here?"

"OK. The security guy is loco, though." He looked in the direction Lynch had gone.

"I hear you. I steer clear of him when I can."

Arnulfo nodded.

"A friend of mine got me this job, helps me pay my student loans," she said.

"My nephew is a carpenter here. He told me they needed a horse man," Arnulfo said.

"A 'horse man?'" she asked.

He shrugged his shoulders. "I asked them if a

cowboy would do." He chuckled.

"And they said yes, I guess?"

"Si."

"Funny." She smiled. "Hey, do you do any work over there by the big shed? By the trucks?"

"The one close to the river? No, not really. Why?"

"I walk by it every day. They keep it locked tighter than a bank vault. Wondered what they keep in there."

"That's where they keep the dynamite, I think."

She stopped brushing the mare. "What?"

"They are going to blast a new road through the rock up there on the ridge, where we ride the horses."

"You don't say."

Chapter 9

"Anything else, sir?" Wyatt asked. An empty bottle of iced tea and crumpled sandwich wrapper lay at his feet. Winford leaned forward gently in his cushioned rocker, staring at the inside roof of the high canvas tent.

Winford had negotiated a commercial loan agreement for their client, Raptor Canyon, LLC. The contract operated in stages, the first requiring proof of title, water rights, corporate structure, and certain minimum investments in the project by the LLC. It also included a host of certifications and assurances by the LLC to the lenders. Winford had been dictating contract forms to Wyatt for nearly an hour and having Wyatt find specific sections in the development agreement for review.

"The certificate of inspection and completion of phase one," Winford finally replied.

"I've not seen a form like that before."

"So it will be your first. Draft up the description and we'll attach it to the signature page, which

I brought with me. The loan agreement requires
two signatures, and we can sign after an inspection."

"I'm not fully clear…"

"Look, Wyatt, it needs to include three things
at this stage – physical access, water supply, and
construction status."

"How detailed?"

"Just that we checked the premises on a certain date, certify that road access to the limestone
ridge is complete, access to the site by foot or horse
is secure, water source is secure, workforce in
place, that kind of thing."

"Got it."

"That's the final document to get us to stage
two, where the lender puts his money where his
mouth is."

"How will that work?"

"The entire project is budgeted at $35 million.
Once the certificate of inspection is done, $10 mil-
lion is transferred to the LLC and the remainder
is available for draw down as needed, a little like a
credit card account."

"So, the LLC only pays interest on what it
really needs, as the project moves ahead," Wyatt
observed.

"Yes," Winford nodded. "The loan agreement
requires the LLC to keep a certain debt to profit
ratio and to keep balances in a contingency fund
that increases slowly over the life of the project but
otherwise belongs to the LLC as part of the loan."

"Then, the company had to finance everything we see around us by itself, here at the site?"

He twirled his finger in the air.

"Yes, Wyatt. All of this, so far, is essentially self-financed by the LLC. But when we're done here, and submit the certificate, all of that is repaid with the initial $10 million deposit." Winford glanced at his watch.

Wyatt closed the document on his laptop and shut it down.

"Schmidt and Lynch will be here shortly. I'll introduce you, then you can be done for the day."

"Yes, sir." Wyatt finished putting his computer and papers into his briefcase and set it aside as the tent flap opened wide. A tall, lanky man entered, his eyes hidden by sunglasses.

"Mr. Schmidt," Winford said, standing and shaking his hand. "Meet Wyatt, one of my associates."

Schmidt gave Wyatt's hand a single, brief shake.

"Lynch is with me," Schmidt said, moving away from the entrance. A stocky man stepped into the tent, nodded, and shook hands with Winford, then Wyatt.

"Have a seat," Winford pointed to two folding camp chairs across from Wyatt. They all sat and waited for Winford to direct the conversation.

"My associate and I are finished up here," Winford told Schmidt and Lynch. "We've finished up the documents that we need to move on to phase two. Wyatt and I will both sign the certificate of completion for phase one."

"Very glad to hear that," Schmidt said with the barest trace of a grin. "We're on track here, but we need that first installment on the loan."

Winford replied, "I know these lenders and their attorneys, Schmidt, and I've gotten them very excited about this project. We're not going to have any problem getting the funding for stage two."

Schmidt nodded and looked between Winford and Wyatt. "Good to know."

"Well, Wyatt, we're done here, so you best finish that drafting work and we can talk again tomorrow. Take a little time off, wander around the camp or go over to the mess tent for some food."

"Yes, sir, thanks." He stood and shook hands again with Schmidt and Lynch, who remained seated.

"See you at breakfast, sir," Wyatt said to Winford as he left.

"Put the tent flap down on your way out, Wyatt."

· · · · · · · · · · · · ·

Chapter 10

Wyatt walked out into the evening air and stretched his back. The sun hung low behind the row of canvas tents, their shadows like bayonets laid across the meadow grass. He started toward his own tent, about forty yards away, then realized he'd forgotten his briefcase. He hesitated a moment, then decided to go back and see if Winford was deep into a meeting with the client or just shooting the breeze. He hoped to listen in, to see how Winford talked to the owners of Raptor Canyon, LLC, to see how the esteemed lawyer worked. Maybe he could even stand outside for a moment or two before announcing that he'd forgotten his computer and papers.

Wyatt moved quietly back toward Winford's tent. He could hear the voices of the men inside and see their vague shapes silhouetted in the dimming light.

"What happened to Cross, your usual associate?" he heard Schmidt ask.

"Out sick," Winford answered. "But Wyatt will sign the certificate along with me, no issues. We'll have our phase two funding in the next ten days."

"Damn good thing," Schmidt said. "If not, we'll be in a world of hurt. The dozer cost twenty percent more than we thought, and that ridge of rock up there has been a bitch to trail through by hand. Any more costs or delays, and you'll need to pony up more cash."

Wyatt stopped and listened more intently. Winford would have to get more cash? Winford was an investor?

"More money from me means a bigger ownership footprint, gentlemen," Winford said.

"To hell with that," Lynch said.

"No, that's the deal. You need more revenue from me, I need more ownership in the LLC. That should be obvious, even to you."

Lynch stood up. "You sanctimonious shithead, you listen to me. You do none of the hard work out here, take none of the risks, and act like you're the boss. You need to adjust your attitude, bub, or I'll do it for you."

"Are you threatening me?"

"Guys…" Schmidt stood up too. "Take a breath will you? We'll make it to phase two without any more money from Winford here, OK? And Lynch, this is a three-way partnership, you know that. Nobody here is the boss of anybody else. Besides," Schmidt sat slowly back into his chair, "Lynch and I got something to show you, Winford, ought to make you smile from ear to ear."

Wyatt could see Lynch's shadow slowly lower back down too.

"Here, Winford, we brought you a photo," Schmidt said. Wyatt could see movement, but their shadows were fading with the sunset.

"What is it?" Winford asked.

"That very special petroglyph panel I told you about. It's all done, right there, a beautiful thing."

The men were quiet for a moment.

"This is going to bring the tourists to this canyon!" Winford said.

"Hell, yes."

"I just wanna be sure about something," Lynch said, leaning forward. "We're never going to tell people this was just some sorta art project, are we?"

"Of course not. This is the real deal. If somebody wants to challenge it, let them. A controversy will just add to the publicity. Most people will want to believe it and that's what counts. Everyone will want to see it, even just to decide for themselves whether it's a fake or not," Schmidt said.

"I've never heard of a dinosaur petroglyph," Lynch said.

"Ever hear of the brontosaurus petroglyph at White Rock Canyon?" asked Schmidt. "The triceratops near Montrose? They've been controversial for years. This new find, right here in our very own 'Raptor Canyon' will charge up everybody for a decade or more. And why not? The rocks are loaded with dinosaur skeletons up in Dinosaur National Park. Why wouldn't the Anasazi come across the same things? They knew a skeleton when they saw one, and they knew a bird skull when they saw one. It's no great leap to understand that they might represent one in their petroglyphs."

"It's our ace in the hole," Schmidt went on, excited. "People should come here anyway as a high-end, luxury retreat. But when they know there's this rare piece of history here to see, a whole panel of it, they'll come in droves. Better yet, they'll be buying high profit tourist crap for themselves and their kids."

"It's a winning concept," Winford said.

"You better say that, you're the one who sold me on this," Schmidt chuckled. "We're going to make Raptor Canyon into its own version of Jurassic Park, desert-style." He handed something to Winford.

"Add this to our trademark application, along with the name 'Raptor Canyon,' would you?"

Wyatt shifted his weight to lean closer to the tent.

"Listen," one of the voices said.

Silence filled Wyatt's ears and stretched beyond what normal conversation allowed. Paranoia flooded from the root of his brainstem, flushed adrenaline through his bloodstream, and pushed the limits of his instinct to flee. His skin and muscles began to overheat and sweat bubbled on his forehead. His breath became shallow and short, his neck and shoulders taut. Could they hear him breathing? Was he casting a shadow across the tent?

The moment stretched onward into the twilight.

"Sure," Winford finally continued. "We'll need a logo too, to add to the actual photo."

Wyatt's muscles relaxed. He took a long, quiet lungful of air and glanced at the sky. The sun flared on the horizon and shadows melted into a deep purple. He turned silently and began to move slowly away from the tent.

"So is this new kid of yours a player?" Schmidt asked.

"Wyatt? Hell, no, he's just filling in for Cross. The kid's a backroom groupie."

"He looks like a smart lawyer to me," Lynch said, "which is why I don't trust him."

"Trust me, the kid's a wannabe, a billing machine. Won't ever be anything else," Winford said.

Wyatt's breath felt hollow as he moved farther away and into the night.

. . . .

Chapter 11

Relic watched as darkness rolled across the canyon like a wave, swallowing the tops of tiny, scattered tents. The northern cliffs, full of bright majesty in the day, morphed into malformed creatures of the night. The sound of a generator reached across the expanse. Lights on poles popped into view along a circus-style tent closer to the river. The soft glow of flashlights moved inside the worker's tents and across the path to portable toilets.

Mechanical clangs and the smell of human sweat had transformed the canyon from the quiet, ancient valley he used to know. The meadows once had been part of a private ranch owned by Cal Snow and his family, used rarely by cattle, even more seldom by mankind. Relic had known Snow, a careful man left widowed with two beautiful granddaughters. He'd bred and trained quarter horses prized by ranchers in four states. Snow had travelled this canyon, knew its secrets, and

kept them. Someone had gotten their hands on
his ranch, or at least this part of it, after he'd died.
Maybe the granddaughters had to sell some of it
off. Some downtown developer got it in his head to
turn the place upside down, build a tourist trap or
a luxury resort, or both, in the middle of some of
the most remote canyon country on the continent.
Like the old song lamented, the developers were
going to pave paradise and put up a parking lot.

Relic shook his head. There were secrets here
in this place. Higher up the drainage, well past
the blocks of sandstone that rimmed the flats,
were cliffs where families lived and dreamed and
breathed ten centuries ago, the ancestral pueblo.
The destruction underway along the river was an
abomination, a curse this canyon did not deserve.
And with it would come hundreds and hundreds
of people every year, beating the grasses to a pulp,
drowning the sounds of crickets at night, driving
the deer and the bats and the ibis far away. And
those people would eventually find the secrets in
this place and destroy them too.

He pulled a plastic flask from his day pack
and unscrewed the top. Tossing his head back, he
took a long pull of his homemade gin, feeling it
burn his tongue and throat and warm his belly. He
put his flask away and put his pack on.

Since the death of the blond man on the
upper plateau, Relic had intensified his observation
of the construction underway, searching the many
faces for the two who had murdered the tool-tot-
ing young man. Somewhere in this melee, he
determined to find tall man and muscle man again.

"Every man has the power of his 'yes' and the power of his 'no,'" he spoke aloud, reminding himself of a saying by an ancient Chinese poet. Time to say "no," he thought. He trotted down a faint game trail and out across the meadow, toward the large canvas tent, the sound of a diesel generator, and the muscle man with a gun.

Chapter 12

Wyatt came to his own tent and stood outside, still stunned by the words he'd heard from Winford. He rested his hand on the center pole and leaned toward the ground, his stomach roiling.

Just a wannabe. Won't amount to anything else, is what Winford had said about him. He could hardly believe it. He'd idolized Winford, and not because he signed Wyatt's paychecks. Winford was a highly respected commercial transactions lawyer. He'd brought billion-dollar clients to the firm, made or saved his clients millions of dollars, probably made the firm millions of dollars. That's what it was all about, wasn't it? Wyatt had been slaving for two years, sixty- and sometimes eighty-hour work weeks, out-performing the hell out of everyone, one of the top billers in the firm. He'd traded a life with friends for a tenth-floor office. He'd lost a girlfriend to the kind of dedication it took to be a success. Todd William Winford, IV, owed him. Winford owed him a lot, and a helluva lot more than the arrogance and disrespect he'd just gotten.

Wyatt slowed his breathing, purging another rush of adrenaline.

It was clear from the conversation that Winford was a private investor and partner in the LLC he represented when negotiating the loan agreement. Negotiations not just for a client, the LLC, but for himself, personally. A clear violation of the rules of professional ethics, the kind of violation that could get him disbarred. With stakes that high for Winford, the potential reward must be enormous too. And a $10 million repayment on his investment, just for starters.

Who else was involved at the firm? Jim Cross, Winford's lead associate? Winford's law partners?

Shit.

He swatted the tent flap out of his way and grabbed his fleece jacket and cap. He turned, ducked back outside, and strode to nowhere with a strange sense of purpose and energy, out into the sage-dotted flats, away from the other tents and into the black of nightfall.

He wandered north for a while, trying to let his mind settle, his feet stepping forward automatically, detached from conscious thought. After a time, a looming presence made him stop and look up. About a mile in front of him, a huge wall of sandstone rose up to meet the stars. Black and immutable, the cliff rim blocked the night sky like dark matter itself. Above the razor-like edge, distant suns and planets sparkled. Below the ragged line of rock, all hope of light was crushed. The feeling was eerie and unnerving…

The air had turned cold, and he put on his jacket and cap. He turned back to look at the glow of lights from camp, surprised at how far he'd walked, suddenly in the mood for a very strong drink. Surely, there would be something to drink in the mess tent.

He tucked his hands in his pockets and started back toward the sound of the diesel generator and the distant sputter of lights above the circus-style tent. Unaccustomed to the dark, he stumbled over rocks and scraped his ankles through the rough sagebrush, slowing his pace.

He could go back to the office tomorrow with Winford, pretend he'd heard nothing at all, apologize for forgetting his computer in his boss's tent. Keep working insane hours. Concentrate on the details of contract terms, deposition transcripts, letters and memos for business dealings, the latest case law and legal analysis. Until he died.

Or, he could go back with Winford, act like nothing happened, then go straight to the other partners, tell them the whole sordid truth. What then? Let the partners fire Winford and accept his fate? Or, would they reward Winford and fire Wyatt?

It all made his head ache. And maybe his heart a little too.

Chapter 13

As he slowed to a brisk walk, Relic tugged a baseball hat onto his head and tucked his hair under his collar. He veered to his right to stay a good distance from the rows of tents. Muffled sounds and lights made the small canvas city seem alive, like electric bees humming inside a hive.

He kept his pace just under a trot, swung a wide arc, and angled back toward the large circus tent under lights on narrow poles. He slowed as he neared the entrance, a large flap of the canvas tied open. At the threshold, he stopped and peered inside.

Two men sat at the far side of the room, talking, and drinking from white plastic mugs. Rows of tables filled the space, folding chairs tucked neatly beneath them. A wide passageway led to a back area partially hidden by portable dividers, navy blue cloth stretched across aluminum frames. He stepped inside.

The two men stopped talking, glanced in

his direction for a moment, then resumed their discussion. He walked casually along the open passage and behind the temporary walls. Directly in front of him stood a long, narrow chef's table made of burnished aluminum. A small, modern-looking kitchen filled the back space. A row of seven refrigerators lined the wall to his left and a long propane stove anchored the far wall. He eased his way toward what looked like supply cabinets to his right.

"Can I help you with something?"

Relic turned to look behind him.

The woman was short but tough-looking, dark skinned, arms on her hips, brown eyes tightly focused on his face. She wore a kitchen apron stained with a dozen shades of coffee, blood, and grease – a Rorschach test for chefs. Black strands escaped from her hairnet and framed her face like party streamers. She stared at him, demanding an answer.

"I just finished changing oil on the trucks. The boss said go try to get something to eat, and tell you I'll mop up the place when I'm done."

She turned her head slightly sideways and glared at him a moment, challenging him.

"Don't bullshit me, mister. You're not part of this crew."

Relic shook his head and glanced at his feet. "No, ma'am, I'm not."

"That's better. I don't hold it against you, that's for sure." She relaxed her stance and put her hands on the chef's table. She smiled wryly. "Can't stand to see a hungry man either." She shook her head.

"Too many years in the soup kitchen not to know when a man's outside the grid, looking for a meal. Sit down, I'll make you a quick plate."

"Thank you." Relic removed his large daypack and set it on the floor. He pulled a stool up to the table and sat.

"But I do expect you to clean up for yourself."

"Yes, ma'am." He touched the brim of his hat.

She gave him a quick, tired smile in reply and hustled back toward the refrigerators. He heard the clank of plates, the whir and ding of a microwave. The cook carried a steaming plate of prime rib, mashed potatoes, and green beans in a white sauce and set it in front of him. He'd forgotten the last time he'd eaten like this.

"Thank you, again," he said, and he meant it.

She smiled a neat row of white teeth. "Take some jerky or something with you, when you leave. Some half-wit ordered enough for an army and it's going to waste." She pointed to cabinets behind him.

"Um hum," he mumbled.

She nodded and turned away.

"Don't you mess up my kitchen, now, 'cause I am beat," she said as she walked away. "Another fourteen-hour day and I am done." She took off her apron, tossed it on the end of the table, and shuffled past the dividers.

Chapter 14

Lynch clenched his jaw as he readied to speak. He had Button, Kowalski, and Cutter with him. "I had a report about workers hanging out in the mess tent last night, staying late when they should be down for the night."

"Heard the same thing," Cutter nodded, pulling his sleeves above his biceps.

"Saw lights on there when I was patrolling the motor pool, last night." Button stretched his left ankle and tapped the ball of his foot on the floor. "Nearly midnight."

"Probably some guys playing poker. Blowing off some steam," Kowalski said.

Button read Lynch's face. "Yeah, but we could tighten things up around here."

"That's right. Past ten is too late." Lynch raised his finger. "And there's no damn excuse for midnight."

"Want us to empty the place?" Cutter asked.

"Yeah, we'll need to start doing that. I'll get

over there tonight and check it out. See who's
hanging around." Lynch narrowed his eyes. "But
we have another issue that's more worrisome."

"Boss?" Button straightened.

"That man I followed with the drone earlier,
he's still out there somewhere, and he probably
works on our staff." Lynch flexed his fists as he
addressed his security lieutenants. "One of the
partners, one of the people financing this project,
is here for a couple of days. We need to keep close
watch for any bullshit. We need to put a stop to
this loose cannon."

Kowalski watched Lynch from under his
brow and crossed his arms.

"What was that guy doing anyway?" Cutter
hooked his thumbs on his belt.

"Spying on us. Watching as we surveyed for
blasting the road."

"How did he get away from the drone?"

Lynch's face reddened a bit. "He might have
shot the damn thing. I thought I heard a pistol shot
but couldn't find the drone anywhere, our best one
too. The guy must have run off with it."

"That's a pretty serious show of intent," Kowalski said.

"That's right. This is not some kind of horse
play. This is not some drunk. You don't do that
without something to hide. I figure this guy works
right here, on our crew. And we don't know what
he's really up to."

Cutter nodded. "Which is why you want us to
look for the asshole."

"I want all of us on high alert tonight. Hide

some of the men on your teams behind the sheds, under trucks, and places a thief might want to break into. Keep your radios hot."

"Description, again?" Kowalski asked.

"Average height, black hair in a pony tail. Tan pants. Runs like a flash."

"There's gotta be a bunch of guys that fit that… except for maybe the pony tail," Kowalski said.

"You couldn't see his face?" Cutter asked.

"Too much motion…"

"Not gonna be easy…" Kowalski shook his head.

"Look into their eyes. If someone avoids you, get on them, follow them and get an I.D. Question them. Detain them if you need to, don't hesitate. A guy named Winford is the visiting partner, and he's key to financing this development. We want him to go home fat and happy. No distractions, no lone rangers stealing our equipment, no problems."

"Got it," Cutter said, patting his sidearm.

Chapter 15

Relic tore into the prime rib like a hungry dog on fresh meat. He groaned with enjoyment at forkfuls of green beans in a sweet, spicy sauce. But in moments, he had to slow down. He hadn't eaten like this in a long while, and his stomach filled quickly.

He lowered his fork and knife and looked around the kitchen. Alone, right here in the heart of the enemy's camp. He might not have another opportunity like this. He examined the inside of the huge tent. A telephone pole held up the high center of the structure. Smaller poles held the ceiling on either side of the center and also rimmed the edges, keeping the canvas sides straight and tight. Ropes inside, and probably outside too, kept the outer skin away from the pole at the center. Many ropes ran from the top to the outer poles, causing the canvas to droop a little between the lines. The main post was probably anchored into the ground and reinforced there.

He rose from his stool, went to the sink, and refilled the water bladder in his pack. He moved to the pantry and opened the door.

"Holy frejole," he whispered. Quickly, he unzipped the main compartment of his pack. Reaching deep into the shelves, he grabbed stacks of teriyaki and barbeque basted jerky, packets of instant oatmeal, two cans of pineapple and a bag of flour tortillas.

That was when he spotted it. On the bottom shelf, his favorite trail food – sugar and protein, sweet and salt, eaten by the handful, chocolate and nuts, in all their glory. Peanut M&M's. Bags of them. He scooped them into his pack until the zipper barely shut.

Smiling at his good fortune, he put his stuffed pack on and went back to his plate. Though awkward to eat with straps on his shoulders, knowing he could leave quickly helped him relax. He chewed his food slowly this time, savoring the beef as only the hungry can.

On the other side of the dividers, out in the dining hall, the men who had been quietly talking stood up quickly, their chairs squealing against the floor. Relic swallowed.

Women's voices carried into the kitchen. A young woman stepped into view. She wore an apron like the cook had and a blue cotton shirt. She wore her dark hair in a bun and smiled while she chatted with her friend, who stepped in after her. The second girl was shorter, her features soft and pleasant. They glanced at Relic, but hardly noticed him at first, bantering back and forth in

Spanish as they made their way to the refrigerators. It seemed like they were part of the kitchen staff.

Relic figured this was about the time to make his exit. Too many lights and too many customers here.

The shorter woman reached into the cooler and pulled out a beer for her friend, then grabbed one for herself.

"Hey," she said with a slight Spanish accent, "do you work here?"

"No, your cook was nice enough to make me a late supper," Relic replied. He pushed the plate away and stood.

"Oh," the tall woman said, taking a swig of beer. She tossed her hair behind her shoulder, narrowed her eyes and looked him over carefully. "You know, you look familiar to me somehow."

"I get that sometimes," Relic replied, keeping his eyes down, making his way toward the passage that led to the front of the mess tent.

Suddenly, a stocky man stepped directly into Relic's path. His mirrored eyes were small but full of fire. He had a sharp chin, a wide forehead, and a nose like whittled juniper. A nightstick and flashlight hung from the side of his belt. A pistol was holstered on his left shoulder. He looked at the young women, then at Relic.

Relic's neck muscles tensed, his fists clenched. This was muscle man, the one who'd murdered the blond guy out on the rise, high in the drainage, in front of the petroglyphs.

Chapter 16

"Lights out, you two," Lynch said to the young women. "Time to close up and move out." They held their beers by their sides and backed toward the far side of the chef's table.

Relic moved directly ahead, nodded at Lynch, and began to pass him. The ladies walked quickly behind Relic, all of them headed toward the main entrance.

"Do I know you?" Lynch asked of Relic.

"Sammy," he replied, hoping there was no real Sammy who'd get into trouble for this. Relic kept his eyes on the ground, rounded the metal dividers, and kept an even pace toward the opening in the tent. The women followed him closely, moving their beers to the front of their aprons, away from Lynch's line of sight.

"What crew are you on? Hey, you, get back here," Lynch called to Relic. He moved to catch up, crowding the women between him and Relic.

****

Wyatt's thoughts ran dark and depressed as he made his way toward the big tent and the glare of lights around it. He stepped quickly to the front entrance, hoping he could buy a rum and coke. Or maybe two or three.

Just then, he collided with a man moving purposefully out of the tent, banging straight into his chest, then practically bouncing off him. The man had a thin goatee of sorts and wore long, black hair tucked under his collar. Behind the man were two women in kitchen smocks who bumbled into the back of the man with the goatee, shouting in surprise.

"Oh, oh, so sorry," Wyatt said, fumbling in front of them.

"Please..." the tall girl said. Then she spied Wyatt and held his gaze, her eyes full of heat, her expression a mix of anger and surprise. Her quick stare turned away, releasing him. He looked past the girl and the man in the goatee and saw Lynch, his face twisted with frustration, his hand on his holster.

"My fault, my fault," the man with the tucked in ponytail said to Wyatt as he pushed past him and out the doorway.

"Stop there!" Lynch shouted, drawing his pistol, pointing it in the air.

The short woman turned toward Lynch and screamed at an absurdly high pitch, her arms and hands shaking like she'd been hit with a tazer, all panic and no judgment. Wyatt jumped backward, out of the tent.

"Put that pea shooter away," the tall woman scolded, her hands on her hips, her lips drawn tight with anger. Lynch held the gun high, ignored the women, and pushed his way between them, his face roasting with rage.

Wyatt's flight reflex rose from his gut and into his throat for the second time that night and, this time, it took hold. He spun on his heel and ran out into the flats, away from the glaring lights of the circus tent, right behind the stranger in the goatee. He stumbled through low sage, tripped and caught his balance, propelled forward by his own momentum until he regained his rhythm and followed the stranger, who was disappearing ahead of him.

"Get back here," Lynch yelled at them. He stopped, raised his pistol at the night sky, and pulled the trigger.

A hard, explosive crack echoed across the canyon, bouncing off the distant cliffs and returning again to Wyatt's ears. Wyatt ran flat out, churning his legs as fast as he could, straight away from the lights of the tents. He was fully in the darkness now, running nearly blind but as steady and as hard as he could. He saw movement ahead of him, a blur that turned sharply to the left. He followed the stranger across an open expanse of hard sand, toward the rumble of water over rocks.

Wyatt pushed his way through a curtain of leaves and dodged through a stand of box elders, touching their trunks and spinning past them. He came quickly to the river's edge and stopped. He bent over, put his hands on his knees and heaved the air in and out of his lungs.

"What the hell are you doing?" the stranger asked.

"Running," Wyatt answered between breaths.

"You're following me."

"No, I just ran," he panted.

"Plenty of room to run out here."

Lynch fired another shot, closer to them. Wyatt could see a beam of light bouncing through the leaves.

"Shit fire," the stranger spat.

Wyatt stared at the oncoming light.

"Only way out," said the stranger. "Follow me. Swim close to shore. Keep your feet up and in front of you, like shock absorbers, in case you hit the rocks." He spun his pack and put it on backward, sliding his arms through the straps, hanging the pack on his stomach. He tucked his hat between his chest and the pack and walked straight into the moving current, black and roiling.

Lynch was crashing through the brush, swinging the light before him. The beam would reach Wyatt's feet in moments.

Wyatt put his hat inside his fleece jacket and zipped it shut. He turned and followed the stranger into the frigid water, feeling the river bottom drop from under him. Soon he was chest deep, treading water as the current swept him past a pile of broken sandstone and toward the roar of rapids.

. . . .

Chapter 17

The river slammed Wyatt into a boulder he
could not see and slid him roughly around it. He
spun a full circle and tried to swim on his back,
with his feet ahead of him, but the current dipped
him suddenly and lifted him again. Waves sprayed
his face and water choked his breath so he kicked
against the water and pulled hard with his arms,
but the rapids did what they wanted with him,
shoving him under, bobbing him back up, spinning him around. He timed his breaths to those
precious moments when his head was above water
but could feel his lungs burning for more oxygen.

In the dark, he had little sense of how fast he
was moving downriver. A long wave carried him
up and, just when he thought he would reach the
top, the crest surged over his head, forcing him to
clamp his mouth shut in mid-breath. Don't drown,
don't die this way, don't let it happen, he thought.
He knew the beach was to his right so he paddled
his feet, swimming harder, aiming blindly toward

what he hoped was solid ground.

Slowly, the waves leveled out and Wyatt caught his breath as he rode into calmer water. He turned himself around in the current and looked back along the shore from where he'd come. He recognized none of it and saw no flashlight or other sign of Lynch. He spun himself again in the water and tried to look downstream. The roar of the rapids began to dull as the river rounded another bend. His clothes were heavy, pulling him downward. His muscles felt sluggish in the icy water and he began to worry about hypothermia. He scissor-kicked his way into a backwater pool, where the current flowed gently upriver. Eventually, his feet touched ground, and he struggled onto shore.

Wyatt turned and sat on the hard, level sand near the water. He pulled his knees to his chest and rested his head in his hands. He tried to take deep, regular breaths, but coughed and hacked a full minute before he could relax.

"So just who the hell are you?"

Wyatt turned and saw the stranger, sitting in the dark a few feet behind him. He looked as thoroughly soaked as Wyatt.

"Shit, man. Way to sneak up on a guy." Wyatt scooted in the sand for a better view. "I'm Wyatt."

"What brings you way out here?"

"I work for Todd Winford the Fourth."

The stranger had returned his daypack from his stomach to his back. "Who the hell is Todd the fourth?"

"A lawyer for the company that's building this

canyon. I'm a lawyer with the same firm."

"No mortal man built this canyon," Relic snorted.

Silence hung between them for a moment.

"Who are you?" Wyatt asked.

"Name's Relic."

"Relic?"

"Why the hell is a lawyer running away from that guy?"

"Lynch. His name is Lynch." Wyatt rubbed his hands up and down his arms to warm them.

"That wasn't what I asked."

"To tell you the truth, he scares the shit out of me. He's one of the partners in the company that's building this resort, and he's chief of security. I overheard some things I wasn't supposed to hear, from him and the two other partners."

"Oh?"

"Look, I'm freezing my ass off here." Wyatt stood. His body jerked and shivered in the cold.

"We're not done running yet, and we're going to have to keep moving or you're right, we'll freeze our asses off." Relic rose and shook his arms and legs.

Wyatt stood, took off his fleece jacket, and wrung the water out of it. Then he began to run in place and swing his arms.

"Follow me." Relic turned and trotted down the hardened beach.

"Better than standing here all night," Wyatt said to himself. He pulled his jacket back on and began to walk, his wet pants sticking against his cold skin. "Hey, slow the hell down a minute…"

Chapter 18

Lynch quickly wove his way back through the box elder and cottonwood trees, away from the river, scanning as he swung the flashlight ahead of him. A crisp breeze rustled through the grass.

There was no sense in chasing those assholes into the freezing water. Those two could deal with rapids and hypothermia, not him.

When he reached open ground, he marched at a steady pace toward the mess hall and then angled east and upslope, toward Winford's tent. By the time he arrived, he was hot and breathing heavily. Schmidt and Winford were standing outside, watching him approach.

"What the hell's going on?" Schmidt asked. "We heard gunshots."

"That was me," Lynch said between breaths. "Caught a thief or a drifter in the mess tent. When he refused to stop, I drew my pistol and shot into the air."

Winford stiffened his neck and pulled his

chin down. "Are you an idiot?"

Lynch's face flushed with anger. "Screw you. I'll have you know that your precious little associate took off with that thief, the two of them, like a pair of jackrabbits."

"Wyatt?" Winford asked. "Why would he run off?"

"Hell if I know, Winford. Maybe he's in with the thief."

"Absurd."

"He's the one who ran, not me."

"You were shooting off your gun like a maniac."

"I'm protecting us. Somebody in this canyon does not belong here."

"You're endangering this project, is what you're doing." Winford jabbed his finger toward Lynch.

"You pissant, I'll take you apart bone by bone." Lynch moved toward the lawyer.

"Hey, hey, you two, knock it off," Schmidt stepped between them. "You, Winford, cool your jets. You don't have the first idea how to run security in an operation like this."

Winford snorted.

"And you," he turned toward Lynch, "need to take a long, deep breath before you start shooting up the place."

"You've managed to chase off my associate, the man who was going to help certify completion of phase one," Winford huffed.

"Hey, your guy was not my concern at all. Like I said, he ran out of the mess tent like he and that thief were together."

"You chased them?" Schmidt asked.

"Right. They were hard to see out beyond the tent lights. But I could hear them well enough and caught them, off and on, in my flashlight."

"So you found them?" Winford asked.

"They ran across the field and into the trees by the water. By the time I got there, they'd jumped into the river."

"Shit," Schmidt said.

"I couldn't follow them."

"Why not?" Winford asked.

"Swimming those rapids is near suicidal. If they don't kill you, hypothermia will."

"Then we have a whole new problem on our hands." Winford folded his arms over his chest. "A dead legal associate is going to bring the sheriff in here and the sort of attention we don't need right now."

"Better a dead one than a missing one," Schmidt said. "If he's missing, there will be a hundred search and rescue types out here, roaming all over the place. We need to find him, quickly, alive or dead."

"How are we going to explain a dead lawyer from your firm," Lynch pointed at Winford, "to the bankers?"

The three men thought about that for a moment.

"He was taken hostage by the thief," Winford said. "That's also why you pulled out your gun, to try to stop a thief in the act but also to stop a kidnapping."

Lynch rubbed his chin and nodded. "They can't stay in that cold river for long, so they' can't go far. I'll get a search party going in the morning."

"Keep it small, just the men you trust," Schmidt said. "To be safe."

"Right," said Winford.

"I just had a dark thought," Schmidt said. "Is it possible Wyatt heard us talking in the tent, after he left?"

"No," Lynch said. "We'd have heard him."

"Shit," Winford stomped his foot. "Don't even think about that."

Chapter 19

Wyatt watched as Relic began an easy lope
downriver, along the beach. Wyatt followed behind, straining to keep up. Relic turned away from
a tangle of branches, still running through the dark
and Wyatt tried to skirt them, too, but tripped,
caught himself, then hurried along. Tall brush
ahead made it harder to see Relic, who blended
with the blackened shapes and began to distance
himself from Wyatt.

"Hey," Wyatt gasped, hoping Relic would hear
him. Wyatt slowed to a crisp walk. He stumbled
over a small log, crashed his ankles through
some sage brush, and stopped to catch his breath.
Searching for light, Wyatt looked up at the stars
and stared. A stark half-moon had risen in the east
and cast a faint light on the ground ahead. Wyatt
could see shapes and vague images, but did not
know if they were rocks, bushes, or nighttime de-
mons. He shivered in the soft breeze and made his
way up the river bank and onto an open field.

"Grab some of that driftwood," Relic shouted.

Wyatt was relieved to hear Relic's voice. "Driftwood?"

"Along the edge of the sand. Carry what you can and follow me."

"I can't see you."

"Follow my voice. There's a spot to camp just ahead."

Wyatt searched the ground but could find no wood at first. He worked his way back toward the beach and found loose sticks, visible against the light sand, and then a long branch the thickness of his arm. He began to drag the log behind him as he scrambled back up to the flats. From there, he moved toward where he'd last heard Relic's voice and walked past a row of tall brush. His running shoes squished water through his toes as he walked, his legs leaden with fatigue.

To his right, Wyatt was surprised to see a flashlight in Relic's hand, scanning the ground around a small alcove.

"You have a flashlight?" Wyatt asked. He dragged the log and carried his bundle of sticks to the base of a low wall of sandstone below where Relic stood. Relic pushed the branches and twigs he'd gathered onto a flat area about five feet above him that formed the bottom of a large bowl of rock. Relic scrambled into the alcove and propped a long log onto the side of the stone wall. Wyatt tossed the small log and kindling onto the sandstone and crawled onto the shelf.

"We couldn't have used the flashlight back there?" Wyatt said with a touch of sarcasm.

Relic looked toward him for a moment but ignored Wyatt's question. He began stacking the wood toward the back of the small alcove.

An icy shiver ran through Wyatt's legs and he began to rub his arms against his body.

Relic finished stacking and carried some smaller sticks to the center of the sandstone bowl, where he sat cross-legged. He pulled his pack close to him, clamped the penlight in his mouth, and laid twigs across each other like tiny logs. He dropped dry grass into the middle of the sticks, rummaged through his pack and pulled out a small plastic container of matches. In moments, Relic had a small fire taking hold.

"Fire," Wyatt mumbled gratefully.

"Hand me some medium sized sticks," Relic said.

Wyatt pulled one out of the stack and broke it with his foot. He handed the pieces to Relic, who gently added them to the flame.

"Find some stones for a fire ring," Relic said, blowing gently on the flames.

By the light of the fire, Wyatt noticed several loose rocks and brought them to Relic, who positioned them around the growing flames.

Wyatt sat across from Relic, warming his hands and feet.

"Well," Relic announced, standing.

"Yeah?"

Relic clapped his hands together. "Time to get naked."

"What?"

Chapter 20

Relic stripped off his shirt and draped it over the branch he had leaned against the wall of the cliff. Then he sat and pulled off his boots and socks. He loosened his laces and placed his boots upside down, near the heat of the fire. He wrung and laid his wool socks on the fire ring, then stood and pulled his pants and underwear off and hung them near his shirt.

Wyatt's face and arms were warming by the fire, but his backside was still very cold. He couldn't help but watch the stranger disrobe in the flickering light of the fire, his movements in and out of shadow, some kind of prehistoric dance.

Relic turned and sat close to the fire again, holding his palms toward the flame. His meager goatee was jet black, his long hair, dark with flecks of gray, in a disheveled pony tail. Skin like dark leather stretched across his wiry frame. Suddenly, he smiled a row of perfect, white teeth. The wild man of Borneo, Wyatt thought. With a dental plan.

"Warming up?" Relic asked.

"Sort of."

"You'd best get naked too, or your clothes will never dry out and you'll be cold all night."

A shiver ran through Wyatt's shoulders and he realized Relic was right. He stood and pried the heel of his shoes off with his toes, laces still tied, the way his parents always told him not to do it, and peeled the wet jacket and shirt from his chest. He wrung them out and slapped them onto the smooth sandstone. He stood and dropped his pants, then his underwear too, rather quickly, feeling awkward in the moment. The air on his skin felt strange and stimulating. He picked up his clothes and walked in his socks to the crooked log Relic had leaned against the rock. He hung his shirt and pants near Relic's and sat back onto the cold sandstone in front of the fire. He poured a cup of river water from his shoes and leaned them against the fire rock, then took off his socks, squeezed them, and laid them by the fire too. He tucked his knees to his chest in a semblance of modesty, and within minutes his whole body was warm and dry.

"Did you say your name was Relic?"

The stranger nodded. He added wood to the fire, scattering its light across his face.

"Where did you come from? What were you doing at the construction site?" Wyatt asked.

"Checking it out."

"Where do you live?"

"Here, in these canyons."

"You live here?"

"That's what I said."

"A ranch around here?"

"No, right here. Where are you from?"

"Denver."

Relic reached into a side pocket on his pack and pulled out a plastic flask. He raised it high and asked: "Want some?"

"Is that what it looks like?"

"Homemade gin. Not bad, if I say so myself." Relic unscrewed the top and took a slow pull on the bottle. He shook his head as he swallowed and made a low moaning sound. "That first one's the sharpest. Here." Relic passed the flask to Wyatt. "This'll warm us up from the inside out."

Wyatt took a mouthful and forced it down. He coughed for a moment, then took a longer swallow.

"Not bad," he said, handing the gin back to Relic.

They sat quietly by the fire for a while, Relic sipping slowly on the tart drink. He handed it back to Wyatt, who took a few more short swallows. The liquor warmed his stomach and reddened his cheeks, making his head spin once around their little alcove.

"Why are you out here, again?" Relic asked, setting the flask by his pack.

"I work for Winford, the lead lawyer who is putting this deal together." Wyatt massaged his bare feet.

"What deal?"

"Developers are going to put up a rustic resort with all the luxuries. A retreat for high-end customers."

"Shee-it."

Relic was clearly disgusted, so Wyatt held his tongue. Relic took another drink from the flask and handed it back to Wyatt.

"OK, you best tell me about these people," Relic said.

"Sure, well, there are three partners." Wyatt's words slurred a bit around the edges. "Winford, Schmizz and Lynch.

"Winford's the lawyer?"

"Right."

"Which one is the body builder? Looks like a weight lifter?"

"Lynch, the one chasing us."

"The tall one?"

"Schmizz. I mean, Schmidt."

"Got it."

"They're partners in the limited liability company – the LLC – that's developing this area. But…" Wyatt crossed his legs and stared into the flames. "I heard something I wasn't supposed to. I wasn't trying to or anything, but I was just outside Winford's tent and they were all in there and I heard them talking…"

"And?"

"I found out Winford, my boss, a partner in my law firm, is a co-owner. He's a partner and has invested maybe several million dollars into the project." He looked up at Relic. "That's not right. That's a breach of attorney ethics that could cost him his career."

Relic nodded and thought for a moment.

"What about Lynch?"

Wyatt's face felt flushed, from the gin or the fire, or both. He took a deep breath. "I didn't think he knew I'd overheard them, but then, at the mess tent, he came at me like he was ready to kill me, and he pulled his gun and started shooting, and so I just ran, on instinct, and you were running too, and I didn't have a clue how to get away from the guy so I followed you." Wyatt's words crowded together in a rush. "Right into that freezing river."

"Hmmph."

Wyatt stared at his hands. "What do you think about all of this?"

Shadows licked across the walls of their shallow cave, stirred by the random flames.

"I think somebody does not belong in this canyon."

Wyatt looked up at Relic.

"And I think betrayal has its consequences."

Chapter 21

Wyatt thought about Winford, Lynch's angry face, the sound of the pistol, the ride through frigid rapids. He watched Relic staring into an unseen distance, then slowly bring his focus home, examine his fingers, rub his hands on his bare legs, and pull his pack onto his lap. "Hungry?"

"God, yes."

Relic began rummaging through the main compartment. The pack looked like it used to be green, but it was too worn to tell for certain. Patches of a different material had been hand-sewn along the bottom. Relic handed Wyatt a thick piece of beef jerky wrapped in a flour tortilla.

"Don't feel like cookin'," he said.

"Don't care," Wyatt replied. "I'll eat anything."

The two men tore into their food. Relic took a long drink from his water bottle and handed it to Wyatt. A tube ran from the bottom through what seemed like a filter of some sort. Wyatt had to squeeze the bottle and suck on the tube to drink.

"So, what's your next move, Denver lawyer?" Relic asked.

"Wyatt. My name's Wyatt." He took another long swallow of cool water and wiped his mouth with the back of his hand.

"So, Wyatt, what's your move?"

"Tomorrow I'll go back to camp. Find Winford and tell him the whole thing, how Lynch chased you and how I got all caught up in it."

Relic snorted.

"What?"

"Lynch will shoot you as soon as he sees you. You'll never get to Winford, and even if you did, why would he help you? You know his dirty little secret. They're all jackasses and if you run with them, you'll become one too."

"Winford doesn't know that I know." Wyatt stopped believing his words as soon as he said them. "Well, maybe."

"You ran. Makes you look guilty as hell."

"Guilty of what?"

"Won't matter."

Wyatt poked a stick into the flame and felt himself pouting.

"I know men like Lynch, and they're danger-ous as hell," Relic continued. "I'd take an honest rattler over men like him, any day."

"How do you know? You don't know Lynch and you don't know Winford. He's a top profes-sional in his field."

"Don't confuse brains for character," Relic said.

"No. If I can talk to him about all this, I can

reason with him, get him out of the partnership, no harm, no foul."

"I know Lynch, and Schmidt too."

"You don't know shit," Wyatt spoke in frustration, kicking his toes against the fire ring.

Relic leaned forward, the light of the fire exaggerating his eyes and cheeks. He took a deep breath. "I saw Lynch shoot a man dead cold, right in front of my own eyes."

"No." Wyatt said. He looked at Relic from under his brow. "When?"

"A couple of days ago. He and Schmidt took a third man to a secluded spot up canyon. Lynch pulled a pistol and shot the man in the chest. I was too far away to stop them."

"Holy crap. You're not joking."

"No, of course not."

Wyatt wondered, not for the first time: who is this guy Relic? What's his real name? His real purpose? Running around these canyons like a hermit, spying on people, watching an execution, or so he says. Is he making this up? Is he a psychopath? Wyatt wondered all these things at once, but something deep inside him could not shake the feeling that Relic was telling the truth.

"You'd have to trust this Winford character to protect you," Relic said.

Wyatt nodded. After what he'd heard in the tent, he knew that trusting his boss was a risky proposition.

Relic grunted.

Wyatt stared at the fire ring. Steam had begun to rise from his socks.

Relic put another branch on the fire. They watched it together as it popped fresh sparks into the air. Two cave men, Wyatt thought, fascinated with the dancing flames, butt-naked on a floor of sandstone. Discussing murder.

Wyatt took a deep breath. He looked above them and could just barely see the top of their shallow cave. Shadows formed and fled around the alcove like nymphs as the fire rose and flickered and shrank, like his thoughts, in a rhythm all their own.

Chapter 22

A wall of russet-colored sandstone rose into the sky across the river, warming gently in the morning glow. Wyatt sat and stared at the sheer cliff, its slick surface broken here and there by crooked ledges and tilted columns. He lay onto his back and pushed himself across the rough stone, scratching a sudden itch between his shoulders. The warmth of last night's fire still radiated from the rocks. He took a deep breath and raised himself onto his knees.

Relic was nowhere to be seen. His clothes no longer hung on the driftwood, but Wyatt's had not been moved. Relic's daypack was gone too, and with it, the food and water.

Wyatt stood slowly and stretched. Here he was, bare as the day he was born, standing in the wide-open spaces for the world to see. The morning air chilled his skin. For a moment though, it felt normal, even comfortable, until he started thinking about the rest of the world out beyond his shallow cave and all the people in it. He gathered his clothes, cold but dry, and pulled them on.

He walked to the fire ring, pulled the stones away from each other, and stirred the ashes with a stick, spreading them to cool. He turned to see a sliver of sunlight appear on the far cliff. Scree the size of pickup trucks accumulated in small piles at the bottom of the huge wall. A rocky terrace sloped from there toward the river, which flowed to his right. A short, gentle plain lay between him and the water. Bushes clipped his view to the left. He scanned the area twice but did not see Relic. He walked to the edge of the small alcove and sat with his legs dangling.

Little had coalesced last night but his anger and distrust for Winford. He had no clue what he ought to do next, but running to Winford for help was now fully out of the question. He would need to find a way out of the canyons and back to the law firm. There, he could decide who to talk to and make sure he still had a future at Reed, Rosen, and Hoyle. He had hundreds of documents to review and index, deposition questions to prepare, work that was piling up while he slept naked in caves and ran around these canyons with a recluse who calls himself Relic. What would a man like that be hiding?

As if reading Wyatt's thoughts, Relic appeared suddenly to his left, parting the bushes and pushing his way through. He looked up at Wyatt and grunted. He removed his pack and tossed up his water bottle, which he'd refilled. Wyatt caught it and took a long, full drink.

"You're welcome," Relic said without rancor.

"Thanks," Wyatt replied. He tossed the bottle back down.

"Here." Relic pulled two pieces of jerky from his pack and a bag of peanut M&M's and threw them toward Wyatt. "Breakfast."

"Thank you," Wyatt said, tearing into the strips of beef.

"So what's your plan, there, mister?"

"Wyatt."

Relic nodded.

"I can't go to Winford about this directly. I think I need to get back to a town, someplace I can rent a car and get back to Denver."

"Back to life as usual?"

"Going back to find out," Wyatt said.

"Well, for now, you can tag along with me if you want to."

"Will it get me closer to a road, or a town?"

"I'll show you. It won't be any farther than going to the highway through the work camp, right past your boss's tent. Which is not your best option."

"So, where to, exactly?"

"Back to the canyon, then up an arroyo to higher ground, east of here, where I can figure what to do next and keep an eye on that little project of yours."

"It's not my project."

"You're helping the man who put it all together."

Wyatt sat silently.

"Grab your stuff. Daylight's burning," Relic

said. He checked and closed his pack then slung it
onto his back and started through the brush.

"Hey," Wyatt said, stuffing the candy and the
rest of his jerky into his pockets. He slid down
the curved stone to ground level and hurried after
Relic.

Chapter 23

Relic led them to a narrow arroyo, about ten feet wide and four feet below the surrounding plain. The dry drainage ran close to, and roughly parallel with, the massive cliffs on the north side of the canyon. Relic launched into a trot that looked easy, but Wyatt worked hard to keep up.

Wyatt was soon dodging rocks and cutting corners to shorten the distance from one turn in the dry creek to the next. Sweat began to run from his brow. Relic pulled ahead and out of sight around the next bend. Wyatt's vision began to narrow to the area right in front of him, and his breathing became more labored. He rounded another curve in the arroyo and looked up the next stretch of the dry creek. Relic had already passed the next turn and was fully out of sight.

"Screw it," Wyatt, said, slowing to a walk and panting heavily. He had to get into better shape, but he was not going to kill himself to keep up with this character. Relic hadn't abandoned him last night, so, Wyatt reasoned, he wouldn't do it now. He'll probably be waiting at the top of this ravine.

Wyatt kept walking at a moderate pace, catching his breath as he went. He moved along a curve to his left, then stopped where it turned abruptly to his right. He stretched his neck back and looked high up along the top of the cliffs along the dry bed. The sight made him dizzy, and he stepped backward to catch his balance.

A distant ringing in his ears slowly became familiar to him. The whine of a small engine seemed to be travelling behind him, weaving in and out of hearing. He turned his eyes from the stark cliffs and searched the blue sky to the south. In a moment, the sound blasted against the high sandstone, echoing in waves. Wyatt moved warily toward the next bend in the arroyo, looking back toward the source of the noise.

A square-shaped drone flew in a straight line toward the cliffs then stopped in mid-air, hovering. Wyatt stared at it for a moment, then turned and ran when the drone moved toward him.

"Lynch. Damn it," Wyatt said to himself as he ran farther up the arroyo and around another bend. He stopped to look behind him, but the sound rose about a hundred feet above him. There, the drone flew in a lazy circle. Wyatt had no choice but to keep moving, but the drone had him now. There was no place here to hide.

Wyatt jogged again, not knowing what else to do. He began to search for a good spot to climb out of the drainage to higher ground. The sound of the drone changed and faded, so he stopped to look.

The drone lowered into tall grass on the level plain just above him. In moments, the throb of a truck engine flooded the arroyo and a yellow pickup lurched to a halt at the edge of the gully, maybe forty yards down the dry creek bed. The engine knocked to a labored stop. Two men jumped from the cab.

Wyatt ran up a slope to the next curve, trying to set a pace he could maintain. The men had a drone, but they could not follow him over such rugged ground in the truck – they would have to chase him on foot. He wondered whether Relic had heard the commotion.

As he worked his way higher, the floor of the arroyo rose closer to the channel walls and Wyatt could see over them in places. He was getting near the end of the drainage, where the ground might level out. He stopped and turned to look behind him. There, coming around the corner at a steady pace, was a man in a blue work shirt with a distinct glint in his eyes.

Wyatt's heart lifted a massive barbell in his chest, pumping suddenly, deeply, washed in adrenaline, his lungs sucking air as he swung away from his pursuer. Sand beneath him shifted with each step, his legs in agonizing slow-motion, one stride forward, a half a stride back, forward, back-slide, forward, back-slide, as he struggled toward the far side of the arroyo and heard the man gaining on him. In the moment it took for him to swing his head to look, all his confidence collapsed, an empty tent without its poles, fluttering to the dirt.

The man leapt onto Wyatt's back and drove

him into the fine gravel. The air blew from his chest like an exploding tire and he lost his sight for a dreadful moment. Instinctively, he swung his right elbow backward, but his attacker was already out of the way. Wyatt pushed himself onto his knees and spun toward the man, panting desperately.

Button held one fist near his chest, the other at his jaw, his legs spread into a fighting stance.

Wyatt got his feet underneath him and struggled to stand. He put his hands on his knees to steady himself and stared at his attacker. He tried to get ready for the next assault.

Button shuffled closer, shifting his left leg forward, then back, showing off. Wyatt raised his fists like a boxer and held his ground. Button moved quickly, feigning an attack. Wyatt lifted his arm to block and when he did, Button slid closer, pulled his leg up and swung his foot toward Wyatt's ribs.

Wyatt stumbled sideways and his side began convulsing in spasms. He forced the breath back into his lungs in shallow gulps, trying his best to stay conscious as Button moved to Wyatt's side, backed into another stance and raised his fists, a wry smile on his tightened lips.

Some fraction of his brain told Wyatt he might soon be dead. His will to survive surprised him, but it seemed his body could do little to help. His stomach knotted in a terrible cramp and he heard himself moan. Out of the corner of his eye, he saw the man moving closer, preparing for another kick.

Chapter 24

Boom! The sound struck his eardrums and echoed through the canyon in baritone waves. Wyatt's attacker screamed in pain, his body twisting in the air in a grotesque pirouette. Then he hit the dirt with a resounding thud and stopped there, suddenly slack and silent.

The gunshot left Wyatt in shock, out of balance, unable to think straight. He sat on the sand, held his ribs, and kept panting for air. Relic appeared in Wyatt's periphery, moving quickly toward Button. Relic watched Wyatt's attacker for a moment.

"He's alive," he said solemnly. "Looks like he hit his head on the ground pretty hard, but a little birdshot to the foot won't kill him." He turned to Wyatt and smiled. "But it'll keep him from kickin' your ribs in for a while."

Relic stepped toward Wyatt and kneeled in front of him. "Let's see if we can get you up slowly." He moved behind Wyatt and slid his hands under

Wyatt's armpits and lifted.

The movement nearly cost Wyatt his fragile consciousness, but he managed to get his feet under him and stand, bent at the waist.

"Easy, get your air," Relic said, steadying him.

Wyatt's stomach began to unclench and his breathing became deeper. His vision broadened, and he could see the downslope of the arroyo, the direction from which they had come.

"That jackass is in shock, but it won't last long. We need to move on outta here," Relic said, moving to Wyatt's right side, sliding under his shoulder and turning him around. He helped him take a couple of tenuous steps.

"Hold up," Wyatt said, forcing them to stop. He leaned forward and waited for another cramp to subside.

"Ready?"

"The drone," Wyatt said. "There's a drone. Where is it?"

"I heard it," Relic said. "But it's not up flying right now. I'd guess the guy working it can't run up this canyon and fly the drone at the same time."

"Humph…"

"Which means we don't have long till he gets here and sets that thing back up in the air. And they find us again."

"Yeah."

Relic took some of Wyatt's weight and they hobbled together toward a side wash that led onto the grassy flat beyond.

Chapter 25

They had slid to a stop at the edge of the ravine, killed the engine, and hopped out. From the black and white images sent by the drone, Lynch figured the man headed up the arroyo was probably Wyatt. Lynch knew Button wanted the chase, loved to test his fighting skills on a real target. Lynch wouldn't mind if Winford's protégé got a meaningful beating.

"Just don't kill him," Lynch had said, not fully sure his employee would obey.

Button had leapt off the edge, down into the draw, and taken off like a Rottweiler after a rabbit. Lynch couldn't operate the drone and follow Button at the same time, so he'd left his eye in the sky in the pickup. Lynch kept a steady pace up the arroyo until he heard what sounded like a light pistol shot. Button didn't have a gun on him.

Lynch reached to his side holster and pulled out his Walther P4, an eight round German pistol he'd had since he was sixteen, and hastened up the drainage, careful not to put himself too much out of breath. He walked at a brisk pace to each bend in the dry bed and peered around the corner before moving on. After nearly ten minutes, he reached the edge of an open area where Button lay on the ground.

"Shit." Was he dead? No one else seemed to be here and the air was quiet.

Wyatt would not have had a gun, would he? No, the guy was a law firm, back-office nerd. That other guy, he thought, the one with the ponytail back at the mess tent. Damn it, this would not go unanswered. Nobody messed with Lynch's crew but him.

Lynch scanned the area around him and moved quietly to where Button lay. He laid his pistol on the ground and checked Button's pulse – erratic, but not weak. A pool of blood surrounded Button's right foot. It looked like buckshot had blended his toes and shoe into a pulpy mass of cloth and sinew.

Button would need to be evacuated to a hospital. The nearest radio and Lynch's drone were back in the pickup truck. Lynch took a handker-chief from his pocket and tied it above Button's foot. He found a short stick and twisted it into the knot as tightly as he could, then tucked one end of the stick into the handkerchief. The makeshift tourniquet would have to do for now.

Lynch re-holstered his P4 and ran back down the arroyo as fast as he could.

Chapter 26

Wyatt began to walk without Relic's help as they crossed slope filled with tiny purple flowers, cheat grass, and brush. They kept a steady pace as Relic led them to a new level in the drainage, one bordered by cliffs with layered bands of tan, coffee, and rust, 500 feet high on either side. The sky widened like an open book. Pale blue along the horizon deepened above him into the reaches of space.

Wyatt's ribs ached and his mind felt numb. He put himself into an automated gait and kept up with Relic's purposeful stride. They walked another half-mile, then came to a great hill made of grayer rock, a hard layer of limestone coursing through the canyon. Relic found some shade at the foot of the hill and sat. Wyatt sat near him on a short rock and caught his breath.

Relic offered his bottle.

Wyatt drank, feeling the warm water washing down his throat.

Relic took back his bottle and took a long drink of his own. He set it down and looked at Wyatt from the corners of his eyes.

It wasn't just his legs, or his ribs, or his pride. Wyatt felt drained of absolutely everything – every bit of energy, every thought, every feeling, every scrap of hope or ambition. He stared at the ground in front of him, seeing nothing.

Relic rummaged through his pack and offered Wyatt a small bag of candy. Wyatt didn't move or speak.

"You know," Relic began with a story-tell voice, "these peanut M&M's are the finest trail snack ever known to man." He tore open the bag. Then he poured a handful straight into his mouth and chewed on them for a while. "Peanuts, you see, provide the protein. The chocolate coating provides the energy. A guy can live on these for years." He looked up and grinned.

But Wyatt was finding no humor on the planet at all.

"That asshole was beating the shit out of me. I couldn't do anything about it." He held his head in his hands. "Helpless," he spoke into the dirt and his stomach heaved.

Relic waited a moment, then patted Wyatt on the back. "Everyone knows helplessness in life, and plenty more than once." He crossed his legs and pulled absently at a tuft of grass. "But you don't know what the next day will bring. Believe me… Helpless can turn to hopeful in a second."

"But it feels like I'm all alone, that I have nothing left," Wyatt said.

"Don't rush to an end game, Wyatt. Take the journey one step at a time."

Wyatt sat up and stared toward the far cliffs. "It feels like I'll never get home, like we're stuck in the middle of nowhere."

"You've got it backward, again." Relic sat straighter. "Stop imagining your life somewhere else for a minute." He met Wyatt's gaze. "We're at the center of the universe here. Right here. We're surrounded by beauty and the spirit of life of this sacred place, above us, below us, all around us, and it will help to heal you back up. Stop ignoring it. Take it all in, one breath at a time."

Wyatt stared at his feet. "Maybe." He looked up again.

Relic leaned forward, put his index finger on Wyatt's forehead, and pushed. "Hit the re-set button, man."

Chapter 27

Lynch struggled up the embankment, grabbing tufts of grass to help him balance. He reached the pickup, walked to the driver's side, and opened the door. Inside, he turned on the radio mounted under the dash and worked the microphone.

"Mayday, anyone at the security center? Mayday."

"This is Stella," a woman's voice crackled. "Identify yourself."

"Lynch. I'm with Button, but he's been shot. We need the medic out here right away and call for an evacuation."

"Say again? Is this Security Director Lynch?"

Lynch repeated his message. "And send Kowalski and Cutter with the medic. When they find Button, Kowalski and Cutter are ordered to follow the drainage higher up the canyon and search for me. I'm going back up now to pursue the intruders."

"Roger that."

"Oh, and Stella…one of the ones who shot Button is Winford's lawyer, Wyatt somebody or other. Be sure all this information gets to Schmidt. Tell him yourself, personally, right away."

"Yes, sir. What's the location?"

"Due north from camp maybe three miles, you'll see the yellow pickup. Button is in the dry creek bed where the truck is stopped, but he's about three-quarter mile east of the truck, up canyon."

"Roger that."

"And Stella…make sure Kowalski and Cutter know the intruders shot Button. They need to be ready."

"Yes, sir."

"I am signing off now, will go back up to Button and then keep moving east. Oh, and I'll have a drone with me. If they see it, the men can follow the drone to find me."

"Roger and out."

Lynch put the microphone back on its hook and turned off the radio. He quickly checked the case that housed the drone and grabbed a water bottle from the truck. He found a sling for the bottle on the floor of the pickup and hung it across his left shoulder, so that the water was on his right.

He ran an initial plan through his mind. He'd get back to Button and check on him again, see if he was conscious or needed water. By then, Kowalski, Cutter and the medic would be close by, driving or riding horses across the canyon from camp. He wouldn't have to stay with Button. He could keep going and then set up the drone to continue searching for the intruders. They'd proven themselves to be dangerous bastards, these two. Who is this guy with the ponytail? He'd find out soon enough. The thought of shooting one of Winford's precious little lawyers brought a crooked smile to his lips.

He touched the holster on his left to reassure himself, took the drone case in his hand, and began the hike back up the arroyo.

Chapter 28

Faye moved her chair deeper into the shade by the mess tent and plopped into it. She looked for any sign of Lynch's security guys and couldn't find any. She slipped a beer from under her apron and held the cool glass to her cheek.

She'd rather take her mid-day break down by the river, shed her work clothes and swim in the icy water until her muscles quivered and her bones numbed. Then she would lie in the sand, her face and sun in a deep embrace, until her ligaments eased back into the warmth of the day. Take a quick nap. That was the right way to do it. But here, security watched all the employees, ever patrolling, moving workers along like they were errant school children. She'd even heard the whine of a drone sweeping over the project.

She twisted the cap and released a hiss of brew into the air.

Across the way, she saw a man trudging toward the front of the mess tent and recognized him. She stood and waved him over.

"Hola," she said.

Arnulfo shuffled tired feet across the ground and into the shade of the tent.

"Here," Faye offered her chair and grabbed another.

"Gracias." Arnulfo dusted off his shirt and sat hard into the seat.

"Another hot one." Faye sat next to him.

"You are not kidding."

She handed him her open beer.

His eyebrows raised, and he smiled a row of gleaming teeth. "Gracias again." He took a long pull on the beer and released a sigh. He handed it back to her.

"Thanks."

"You could get fired for drinking that," he said.

"Wouldn't mind it, actually." She took another swig and handed it back to him.

Arnulfo held the bottle for a moment then poured another drink down his throat.

"Here, the rest is yours," he said.

She nodded and finished the beer with two quick swallows.

They stared out across the canyon, listening to the sounds of a backhoe on the other side of the tent, watching a pickup truck full of lumber easing across the uneven ground.

Just then, a man with a "Security" t-shirt walked around the corner of the tent. Faye rolled the empty bottle away from them. He shaded his eyes to see them and nodded, then he turned away and disappeared.

"He'll be back in two minutes to make sure we're not lollygagging," Faye whispered.

"Si."

"What the hell is all this going to look like when it's done?" Faye asked.

Arnulfo sat in silence for several moments. "Big complex. Hotel, restaurant, horse ranch…"

"They've dug two trenches and filled them back in since I've been working here," Faye said. "They are ruining this beautiful canyon and don't even seem to know what the hell they are doing."

Arnulfo grunted in agreement.

"I'd be happy to see this whole mess burned to the ground."

"People like these people, they don't stop what they are doing. They will finish this."

"I'd still rather roast marshmallows over it all."

Arnulfo smiled. "Then I will join you, my friend."

The security man strolled back into view and cast a glance toward them.

"Until then, keep your head low," Faye told him. She stood, brushed off her apron, and went back into the heat of the kitchen.

Chapter 29

Wyatt had lost track of how long they'd been sitting there in the shade. He could feel the shock of the kick boxer's attack fading slowly, a more and more distant echo. He reached for the bag of candied peanuts and put two in his mouth. The sweet taste of chocolate drew his attention to the crunchy mass and he began to masticate with more focus than he expected.

"Told you so," Relic said with a grin.

Wyatt smiled and swallowed. He grabbed four more.

"We need to get to water." Relic sloshed the last of the liquid in the bottom of his bottle.

Suddenly very thirsty, Wyatt nodded.

"See those lines up on the boulder?" Relic pointed to the rock behind Wyatt.

Wyatt turned. Three wavy lines were etched into a large sandstone rock, all about chest height.

"Petroglyphs?" Wyatt asked.

"Yes. Ancient pueblo used them for many

things, including maps and directions."

"Anasazi? I've heard of them."

"Ancestral Hopi, to be more accurate."

"Maps?"

"Sure. Maps, markers, reminders of key events or resources, like water."

"Ingenious."

"Indeed."

"How do you know so much about these lands, and petroglyphs?"

"One of my grandfathers was Hopi. He used to talk about how our ancestors roamed and built their communities all through these canyons. They irrigated, grew beans, squash, and corn. They domesticated dogs and turkeys. Designed kivas and community centers and multi-story apartment complexes and military look-out towers. They placed granaries in strategic spots across the land so they had food and water as they hunted and traded with other towns and tribes." Relic waved his hand toward the sparse meadow and distant cliffs.

Relic seemed more talkative than usual, and it whispered a question in Wyatt's ear. Am I so close to shock, or in such poor condition, that Relic thinks he needs to keep me talking? Relic was inscrutable, but a man with no ill will, a man Wyatt began to think of as a friend.

Wyatt looked around him, up at the jumble of dark rock mounded behind them, across the open ground to the far wall of sandstone, along the knife-edged rim and into the deep sky.

"To some people, this place looks lonely and

desolate," Relic continued. "But it's full of life and history. It's connected to the ancient ones, and they to it, and us to all of them. It's full of meaning here."

"You would never know this is up here," Wyatt said. "I mean, looking at the canyon below us where everybody is camped. It's a whole other level. From down there, it looks like the dry creek just peters out, but then this meadow opens up and these cliffs start to come together and it's a whole other world."

"Wait till you see what's next."

"Oh?"

"I want to ask you a favor first, Wyatt. I want you to agree not to show anyone where I'm going to take us now, to get water."

"Well, sure. Who would I show?"

"These canyons only stay safe if people like your boss don't know about them, can't exploit them."

Wyatt nodded. "Not sure if he's still my boss…"

"Then let's get going." Relic stood and stretched, then began a brisk walk along the base of the hill.

Chapter 30

Lynch found Button sitting up against the side of the arroyo, tightening the homemade tourniquet above his ankle. Button waved at him with a visible sense of relief.

"Glad to see you awake," Lynch said.

"Glad to be awake. What the hell happened?"

"You got shot in the foot."

"No 'duh,' boss, but who? The lawyer didn't have a gun, or he would have drawn it on me."

"Must've been the guy with a ponytail, the one I chased out of the mess tent last night. The two of them ran off together, down to the river, where I lost them. They must still be working together."

Lynch let Button take a long drink of water.

"I'm going after them. The medic will be along shortly, with Kowalski and Cutter. They're going to make sure you get out of this canyon and to a hospital to look at that foot. Then they're going to follow me, for backup."

"Tell them to shoot that bastard in both feet before they kill him."

Lynch grinned. "I'll do worse than that."

Button nodded.

"Help should be here any minute, so I'm going to keep moving."

"Go get 'em, boss."

Lynch grunted an affirmation and put the water back into his sling. He turned and began at an even trot.

He soon passed the next corner of the meandering wash and noticed the drainage walls become lower and lower. The arroyo was widening and petering out. He looked left and right as he went, slowing his pace. Ahead lay a tall jumble of broken rock. He guessed that the intruders would keep moving, though there seemed to be little left of the canyon.

Lynch worked his way awkwardly through and over the boulders, keeping the drone case in his left hand. After a while, the rocks began to clear, and he found a wide, flat meadow of sorts. Green grass and sage dotted the small plain. To his left, golden cliffs of banded sandstone rose high in the air. Across the way, similar cliffs angled toward him, tightening the canyon to an area about a mile wide. He walked toward the near-side cliffs and a row of boulders at their base. Spotting a game trail that rose a few yards uphill, he decided to follow it.

The path leveled out at the top of a flat boulder. His view of the canyon was good from here, so he sat crossed-legged as far out on the rock as was safe and unlatched the case. He removed the drone, checked the camera, microphone, and propellers, and set it aside. Then, he opened the console and powered up the controls.

Within minutes, he had the drone in the air and tested its maneuvers. He began to fly straight across the canyon to the cliffs on the other side. When he reached the sheer sandstone, he turned and worked his way in a zig-zag pattern to a spot just above where he sat, then repeated the process, moving ever east. No one was going to slip through his fingers.

Chapter 31

Relic wound his way through a jumble of ankle-wrenching stones, darker and sharper than the sandstone that dominated the rest of the canyon. He stopped and searched the hillside from time to time, scanning ahead and behind him.

Wyatt's juiceless tongue stuck to the side of his mouth like skin on a dry ice cube. He pulled it loose and hoped like hell the water was near at hand.

"There," Relic said, pointing a few yards ahead.

A hillock of angled stone lay before them, but no sign of water.

"Here?" Wyatt asked.

"The entrance is over there."

"Entrance?" Wyatt stumbled over a rock and caught himself.

Relic moved quickly toward the knoll.

A distant, high-pitched sound teased at the edge of Wyatt's awareness and he stopped. The noise disappeared, and he thought it must have been a ringing in his ears. Relic had moved close to the small hill and seemed to be examining it. Then, the whirring sound resumed, clear and distinct this time, moving toward them at a high speed.

Shit. The drone they'd heard earlier was back, hunting them. His stomach clenched.

"Relic," Wyatt shouted. He ran toward Relic and yelled again. "Drone!"

Relic turned toward Wyatt and nodded, then began moving rocks from the side of the hill, rolling them away.

"What are you doing?" Wyatt asked.

"Dig. Help me dig these rocks away."

Wyatt stood over Relic, unsure where to begin. The metallic buzz drifted away for a moment, then grew louder and louder.

"Here." Relic slipped between the stones and disappeared. "Follow me," he shouted, pushing another rock out of the way.

Wyatt looked up at the sky but could not spot the hovering craft. He moved closer toward the hillock and found where Relic had slipped into the earth. He searched the horizon one more time but could not find the flying machine. Suddenly, the shrill noise began to echo again against the cliffs, clamoring across the sky in desperation, seizing Wyatt's breath as it drove him into the crevasse.

The drone hovered high over Wyatt as he disappeared.

Chapter 32

Wyatt squeezed through an opening the size of a refrigerator and pivoted to his right. A spacious room opened before him, the ground flat and hard-packed. Sunlight bounced off the rock walls and, as his eyes adjusted, he could see most of the cavern laid out before him. Relic sat to one side, searching through his daypack.

Wyatt walked across the floor and sat next to him. "What is this place? How did you know about it?"

"It's a natural cavern the old pueblo people used as a temporary shelter and a source of water." Relic pulled a headlamp from his pack and put it on. "Over there." He pointed with the light.

"Jars?" Wyatt asked.

Seven archaic clay pots lined the far wall, fat-bottomed with narrow necks and handles. He could see black on white designs across four of them. Earthen bowls were laid out next to the pots and spoons made of sheep horns next to the bowls.

A fire ring anchored the center of the room, the stones blackened from ancient fires.

"Pottery," Relic replied.

Wyatt leaned forward for a better look. "How old?"

"Old as man himself." Relic scanned the cave with his headlamp. "Over there," he pointed again, "is a set of bow and arrows and a leather bag full of chert for making knives and scrapers. Next to them is a perfect set of sandals and a child's doll made of deer hide and shells."

Wyatt walked on hands and knees to the fire pit and peered into it. Remnants of charred wood and small bones lay scattered inside the circle.

"Please don't touch anything."

"No, I suppose not."

"These are preserved just as the people left them, thousands of years ago. Stored here for when they were needed. Weapons, tools, probably dried corn and beans in the granary over there." He turned his head to the right and his headlamp lit a waist-high stack of rock and mortar.

"Incredible."

"Great place to get out of a storm or hide from enemies. Rest and recuperate. And the water…"

"Yes, we need water."

"…is down there a ways." Relic looked deep into a sudden dip in the cave a few yards from where they sat.

"How do you know about this place?"

"The rancher who owned this canyon showed me when I was a teenager. I don't come into the

cave very often, and when I do, I stay to this side of
the old living area, to keep it undisturbed."

"It's like they just left, like, only a few minutes
ago," Wyatt whispered.

Relic turned off his headlamp and looked at
him. "That's right," he said, a note of appreciation
in his voice. "We're their unexpected guests. They'll
be back any minute with fresh meat and tall tales
for everyone."

Wyatt pulled his knees to his chest. "It's like
we're sitting in their living room."

"It's not like any museum," Relic looked
across the expansive cave. "History is right here,
right now, in this place. No displays, no velvet rope
bullshit."

Wyatt noticed the faint scent of ash and
leather stir across the cave. Relic was right. We're
as much a part of human history as they are, all
of us here together, all at once, no boundaries.
No placards to read, no instructions to follow, no
glass-encased exhibits to examine. No florescent
lights buzzing in the back of your head. This is the
real deal, the world still firmly hinged to itself and
to history, still flowing as if a thousand years was
nothing at all, just the day before yesterday. They
were in it here and now, as alive and alert as the
ancients.

He heard only Relic's measured breath, and it
seemed like the rhythm of time itself.

Wyatt blinked some moisture from his eyes.

"Well," Relic cleared his throat. "We'd better
get to water now and hope that drone didn't see
us find the cave." He reached into a pocket on his

pack and handed Wyatt a flashlight the size of a thick pen. "Not the greatest, but the only extra I have."

"Thanks."

Relic stood and put his pack back on. Turning, he lit his headlamp and moved carefully down a crude set of stone steps. As they descended, the diffused light of the living room faded to a pinprick far above them.

Chapter 33

Lynch landed the drone on a flat spot of ground several yards from where Wyatt had disappeared into the hill. There had to be a cave of some sort there. He packed up his gear and stood on the high rock where he'd been sitting. He could see the change of rock up ahead, where sandstone gave way to something darker and harder. He searched across the canyon floor and behind him, but saw no sign of Kowalski or Cutter. If they followed orders, they'd eventually reach this high canyon, but he did not want to wait for them.

He worked his way back down the thin game trail to level ground and walked quickly along the cliff toward where he'd landed the drone. After twenty minutes, he realized he'd passed the spot and doubled back. This time, he saw the drone easily and went to pick it up.

He turned the aircraft over in his hands, examining the frame and props. It seemed to be in good shape. He carried it to the base of the hill where Wyatt had disappeared and laid the drone and its yellow carrying case on the ground. He pulled his P4 from the holster and searched for the entrance to a cave.

After several trips along the hillside, he noticed a tall crack in the rocks and moved slowly into it. Cool air blew across his face as he moved farther in. He heard nothing and leaned carefully into the cave. When his eyes adjusted to the dim light, he saw an old fire pit and some pottery and other stuff scattered along one wall. But the footprints in front of him were fresh. They led deeper into the cavern and out of sight.

Lynch holstered his pistol and slid quietly back outside. He moved the drone to an obvious spot on the rocks, where Cutter and Kowalski could find it, right in front of the entrance. Then he unlatched the briefcase and rummaged through it until he found a compact flashlight in an inside pocket. He closed the case again and placed it on another rock within sight of the drone. He tested the flashlight then worked his way back into the hillside crack.

Once inside the cavern, he walked on the balls of his feet to the edge of the light, where rough stairs, of sorts, led deep into the dark. He saw a single boot print on the first step down and, so far, this was the only way forward. He listened closely for any sounds, but heard none. They must be a good distance away, and maybe around a bend too. He held his light at the ready and tested each step carefully as he slid his way into the black.

Chapter 34

By the light of Relic's headlamp, they crossed a concourse of sharp boulders the size of chairs and tables, a field full of foot-snaggers and ankle-wrenchers. More or less level, the tangle of broken rocks led gently to their left and finally ended at a ledge of rock by a giant entrance. The air had become damp and heavy with the smell of mud. Wyatt could see a high ceiling above him when Relic looked up with the light and, though the darkness closed in on him, Wyatt took comfort that the cavern was large and open.

They stood under an archway of sorts and looked around. Wyatt could smell the water ahead of them.

Relic swept the ground with his light and moved across the level ground several yards. He stopped suddenly in front of a pool so motionless it seemed like a coat of gloss poured over the bedrock, a desert mirage in reverse. They kneeled at the shoreline and Wyatt followed Relic's light as it searched the new cavern.

Dry ground circled to their right into a maze of cracks and crags in the gray limestone. To their left, the water ran to a solid rock wall maybe two stories high. Relic's light could not reach the far side of the pond. He shined the light directly into the pool and they stared deep into liquid clear as air. Wyatt cold not tell how deep it went. Rocks that looked the size of basketballs could be as big as dump trucks, for all he knew. Depth perception was useless and gave him an upside down feeling as he stared into the deep pool.

Relic took the water bottle from his pack and removed the filter that hung under the lid.

"This water's good to drink straight up." He shook the filter and put it in a side pocket. He dipped the bottle gently into the pool, sending ripples that warped their view of everything beneath the surface. Wyatt sat on the ground and watched Relic drink the entire bottle and then refill it. He then handed it to Wyatt.

The icy water burned like hot soup down his throat then coated and cooled his mouth with relief. He hadn't realized how dehydrated he'd become until then. He stopped to gasp for breath and then took another long drink.

"Here." Relic handed Wyatt a flour tortilla and a stick of barbeque jerky. "Courtesy of the mess tent."

They ate hungrily and washed it down with more icy water. When he thought he could eat no more, Relic offered him a handful of candied peanuts. Wyatt could not resist.

They sat resting for a while, letting their quick meal settle in.

"I thought I'd be really nervous in here, but this is OK," Wyatt said. "It feels safe."

"Let's hope so," Relic nodded. He filled the water bottle again and tucked it into his pack. He turned his headlamp off.

Tiny white needles flashed briefly on Wyatt's retina, remnants of light fading as blackness filled the cavern. At first, he thought he could still see Relic, sitting two feet away. But as he tried to discern his companion's shape, he realized that he'd lost all measure of sight to the deep obscurity.

"Whoa."

"Shh, listen," Relic said.

A distant clack of rock on rock reached Wyatt's ears. Then, something made him turn his head toward the long pile of stones they'd scrambled across to reach the water. There, ghostly and faint, was a cast of light bobbing across the cavern wall.

Chapter 35

Relic stood quickly and put his pack on in the dark. Then he turned on his headlamp and faced across the sheen of water, deeper into the cavern. Wyatt's heart began to pound, and he leapt up and grabbed Relic's arm for a moment.

"This way," Relic whispered. Wyatt reached down and felt the penlight through his pocket, but the weak reassurance was a consolation prize. He followed Relic as they walked briskly to their right and along the edge of the water into the recesses of the cavern.

The blackness seemed even more complete near the back of this part of the cave, their world defined entirely by the weak light of Relic's lamp. They crossed an open area for maybe forty yards. Two vertical crevasses opened to their right, parallel to each other, several feet apart. Relic examined the nearest crack carefully, peering into it and ducking back out. He moved to the farther opening and shuffled part way into it, his light shrinking to a blade the size and shape of the crevasse. He wiggled back out.

"I'm pretty sure this is it," Relic said.

"Pretty sure what is what?" Wyatt's voice raised an octave.

"When I was young, we found more rooms past a narrow crack in the wall. I'm pretty sure it's this one, the second crack." He kept his voice low.

"Shit."

"Follow me." Relic looked to the ground so they could see where to step, then turned back into the crevasse and looked up. The fissure was huge, leading way above them and beyond where light could travel. He looked down again and shuffled his feet along the floor.

Wyatt tried to watch the light in front of Relic to anticipate where he would need to step. As Relic moved along, the crack opened wider but the floor became a thin ledge jutting out from the left side of the near-vertical wall. Relic leaned his chest into the side of the rock and placed one foot directly in front of the other, grabbing handholds where he could find them. To their right, the ledge dropped into an abyss Wyatt could not imagine.

He turned his stomach to the wall and kept his eyes facing right, watching and doing as Relic did. He shuffled his feet along the scant ledge, feeling for hand grips. Suddenly, his right foot slid off the edge, his weight pulling him down to a crouched position. He bounced once on his supporting leg, dead weight on a shock absorber.

The air blew from his lungs in a single "humph," and he squatted there, balanced for just

a moment. He waved his hands along the wall,
searching desperately for a hold when his other leg
slid from beneath him, twisting out into the open
depths. He clawed against the cliff but his fingers
could not hold against the sudden drop. Sharp
rock scratched and stung his arms as he reached
for something, anything to stop his fall. His elbows
slid and then cracked against the ledge and he
tightened his biceps, keeping the top of his head
just above the narrow path.

"Ugh," Wyatt panted, his feet kicking and
tugging him deeper into the black space beneath
him, no place for balance or rest.

Chapter 36

A fiery brightness blinded Wyatt's eyes.

"Here." Relic reached for Wyatt's right hand. They gripped each other above their wrists. Relic groaned as he lifted Wyatt's weight with his legs. Wyatt raised his right knee onto the ledge and took a breath. With Relic's help, Wyatt stood slowly on that leg, pushed himself against the rock wall, and got his left leg under his weight.

Sweat dripped down his temples as Wyatt tried in vain to calm his pulse. Relic turned away, swinging the light back into the crevasse.

"Not much farther," Relic said, moving carefully along the ledge.

Wyatt slid his feet across the path, feeling the lumps and slants as he went, being sure to have two handholds for every step forward.

Before long, the ledge widened again, and he walked more quickly around a gentle bend and out into another chamber.

Watching Relic's light bounce around the

room made Wyatt slightly nauseous.

"Stop," Wyatt panted. "Show me a place to rest. Please."

Relic scanned the ground until he found a stool-sized rock. Wyatt used the light to climb on top and rested his back against the wall of the cave.

Relic resumed a short survey of their surroundings. They seemed to be in an egg-shaped bubble in the mountain, the sides of the cave curved toward the floor. A scattering of sand and pebbles were deposited at the lowest point in the room. Two tunnels, of sorts, exited the chamber above them, but they could not see how deep the passages were.

Relic wandered to where Wyatt sat and joined him a few feet away. His headlamp flickered suddenly and dimmed. Relic tapped it and it brightened again.

"Better turn this off for a while," Relic said, submerging them into nothingness.

A wave of vertigo spun Wyatt's head like a circus ball, dropping him up and lifting him down. He squeezed his fingers against the rock, trying to anchor his mind to something, anything stable. Quiet wrapped his head like a woolen blanket, smothering his senses, absolute and unrelenting. Wyatt thought he must be a thousand feet below the sea, imprisoned in dark currents, pressurized into a tight, immobile shell of skin, his brain rubberized by fear. Already mildly claustrophobic, a panic rose within him he'd never felt before. He began to wheeze, his breath rattling like a child slurping his straw in an empty glass of milk.

"Wyatt." Relic reached over to pat his arm.

Wyatt jolted at the touch and gasped.

"Hey, we're OK," Relic said. "We'll figure it out."

"Don't bullshit me."

"Right, then. No bullshit."

Wyatt nodded in the dark, out of habit.

"Focus on your breathing for a minute. Breathe in through your nose and out through your mouth. Take your time, you're in no hurry," Relic said.

Relic's voice was deep and reassuring, a point of human contact he suddenly treasured. The circus ball in his head began to slow its spin, and he tried Relic's suggestion, breathing in, breathing out. He began squeezing and loosening his hands against the rock and it helped him find a sense of gravity.

"What are we going to do next?" Wyatt asked.

"We're going to take a break. We'll figure it out in a little bit. For now, think about your office, your best girlfriend, or playing baseball, or sitting around the fire."

Wyatt closed his eyes at the thought of going back to his office. His vertigo returned in full force, spinning his body inside itself, tossing his thoughts with hurricane force. He lay onto the rock as if it were a meteor hurtling through the black of space.

"Come on, Wyatt, you gotta have something you like to do. I bet you play squash or golf or something like that. Tell me."

"No." He pressed his cheek to the stone. "Some basketball on Sundays, just a pick-up game."

"There you go. You any good at defense?"

"Lousy. It's just a diversion."

"What do you work at the hardest?"

"You're not fooling me, you know. You're just trying to keep me talking."

"Is it working?"

"It's annoying."

"Well, maybe it's my turn."

"Huh."

"Then tell me about your boss, this Winnie-ship fella."

"Winford."

"Right."

"The fourth."

"No shit?"

"Really."

"Parents got no creativity, huh? Make a guy take the same name four times in a row?"

"Yeah, I guess so." Wyatt sat up slowly and rested his back on the wall again.

"So, what's he like to work for? Does he treat you good, piss you off, lose his temper?"

"He's an odd one. Rigid most of the time, prim and proper, but like it's all bottled up inside. He can lose it too. I heard talk around the office that the other partners made him take an anger management class once."

"I bet that really pissed him off."

"Huh." Wyatt chuckled once, then again, then it rolled off his tongue in waves, pulling Relic with him until laughter displaced the empty cold and echoed through the chamber.

. . . .

Chapter 37

A faint flash of light and the sound of boots on hardscrabble brought their moment of humor to a grinding halt. Wyatt held his breath. Relic switched on his headlamp, now wavering under tired batteries.

"Time to go," Relic said.

"There's no place left," Wyatt said. "We have to stay here and hide or fight it out."

"No. There's another move ahead of us and we'd best take it." Relic stood and walked across the cavern to the other side and began to examine the far wall and an open tube, of sorts, above it.

Wyatt willed himself to stand and shuffled carefully across the curved floor to where Relic stood. He could hear the crisp sound of feet crunching on gravel, the occasional grunt of effort back in the crevasse. Lynch wasn't trying to be quiet, Wyatt realized. Lynch wasn't hiding his approach because he was confident he could eliminate both of them. He and Relic, entombed in these caves forever. Wyatt shivered.

"Here's the deal," Relic said, removing his pack and searching inside. "I'll go ahead. If it's passable, you follow me with your light."

Wyatt stared into the dark entrance. "You're shitting me."

"No, we agreed. No bullshit."

Wyatt's heart pounded in his temples.

Relic took a length of nylon rope and tied one end to his daypack, the other to his belt. "I'll pull this behind me. If it gets stuck, you can get it loose."

"We have no clue where that will lead us."

"Our only choice is to see if we can make it, or die here."

"You have a pistol, let's hide and use it."

"This room is wide open, no place to hide. My headlamp's going out on us. Besides, all I've got in my gun is buckshot. If we can get to another chamber, one with some cover..."

"We could go back into the crack, catch him on that ledge…"

"He'd be past it by the time we got there."

"Relic. This is crazy. Listen to me…"

But Relic was standing on rocks below the tube, reaching into it, his headlamp searching deeply, leaving the cavern black. Wyatt reached into his pocket and fumbled with the penlight, panic rising again. He felt the switch and turned it on. A weak glow lit the back of Relic's boots as he struggled into the tight passage. In moments, his daypack lifted behind him, then stuck. Relic squirmed backward, tried again, and the pack jammed behind a knob of rock at the base of the tunnel. Wyatt heard Relic's muffled voice and remembered to lift the pack and push it along. Relic's boots scratched the sides of the passage as he moved ever deeper.

Wyatt held the penlight up to the tube, watching Relic's feet slowly disappear into the dark.

"Ah, damn it," Lynch said.

Wyatt heard the words float just within hearing and fade away. Lynch was in the middle of the crevasse, maybe having some trouble. But once he got past where the ledge narrowed, he would make good time the rest of the way. He was probably only fifteen minutes, or less, from where Wyatt stood.

Never had Wyatt faced such a choice. Here, in the cave, at least he could move, could breathe. Lynch would kill him or, worse yet, wound him and leave him to die. But ahead lay what looked like his own stone coffin, hard, cold, forbidding.

A mixture of sand and tiny stones slid along the bottom of the passage and poured into the cavern. He peered inside the tube and heard Relic's faint voice saying something, "here," maybe. He couldn't make it out. But he had to decide. Die here. Go now.

He clamped the penlight between his teeth, stepped onto a higher rock, and leveraged his arms and shoulders into the shaft. He found a solid hold and pulled himself in like doing a chin-up. From there, he wiggled his arms forward again and could feel his shoes touching the edge of the passageway. He was in.

Saliva dripped down his chin as he tried to keep the penlight in his teeth. Ahead, he saw only a funnel of rock disappearing into a solid wall of earth. But he knew Relic was up there. Somewhere.

Wyatt tried to pull his knees up to his stomach, but it was no use and a flush of panic fired his cheeks. He was going to have to wiggle through the tunnel like a worm. He took a shallow breath and pushed with his toes and pulled with his fingers, dragging his chest and legs.

Progress came in inches. He stopped for a moment to take the light from his mouth and hold the lamp farther up the shaft. The slope of the tunnel stayed about ten degrees all the way out of sight. It didn't seem to look any worse up ahead. He just had to keep at it.

He wiggled and pulled himself along, making some steady headway. A small rise in the passage crowded his stomach against his ribs, then dropped away as he slid past it. The flashlight balanced between his thumb and forefinger and shook with each movement of his hand. It seemed to be fading. Was he imagining it? Should he turn it off for a while?

A sharp hook of rock latched against his belt and he was suddenly stuck. He tried to bend at the waist, to pull himself off, but his rear was tight against the roof of the shaft. Then he twisted, but that only tightened the hold. He pushed his toes against the tunnel and pulled as hard as he could. Panic hit him again, shuddering through his body, crushing his brain into mush. He lay there barely breathing, stuck like a piece of gristle in the devil's gullet.

Chapter 38

Wyatt tried to believe there was some hope, some way out of this unmovable, unforgiving passage, but he did not believe it. Despair threatened to stop his heart altogether. If it did, he decided he would not resist.

He took a slow breath in through his nose and let it out through his mouth, remembering Relic's advice. He began to count each breath, one, two, ten, fourteen.

He focused on a half inch scar in the limestone tunnel, inches before his eyes. A giant feature in this cramped universe, Wyatt began to wonder what made the uneven shape, what darkened it against the surrounding stone. Maybe it was an ancient fossil, or a slice of mud left by a snail in the sea floor, millions of years ago. It needed a name, like the names of craters and mountains on the moon. Maybe he could name it after himself – the Mighty Wyatt Trench, the Colossal Wyatt Mudslide. Sure. He would name every peak and valley in this Gulliver's Travels landscape and memorize their locations. Would that keep him sane? Or was it a signal that he was already over the edge?

If he stayed here long enough, his thoughts would disintegrate into eternal gibberish.

He realized what he had to do. Counter to his objective, in terrible conflict with his instinct, he had to…back up. He lifted his weight onto his toes and pushed with his hands, sliding back down the uneven shaft. Then he twisted to his left and worked his way back up again, trying to keep his belt off the bottom of the passage. After several minutes, he decided he was past the trouble and shifted to a more even position. He looked around the rocky shaft. He'd lost the formerly massive Wyatt Trench – he'd moved beyond it.

He decided that his light was, indeed, fading. He pulled himself farther up, reached his arms out again, and flicked off the light. He said a silent prayer that it would come on again when he needed it most.

Wyatt pushed and pulled again, moving several inches up the slanted tube. He searched ahead for any sign of anything, but all was black and quiet. His fingers felt the tunnel in the dark and grabbed another small hold. He slid another few inches forward.

He pushed against the sides of the tunnel and pulled, like a truncated breaststroke, dragging his body forward. His arms ached, and he pushed again with his toes, gaining another length.

To his great relief, there appeared a gentle glow.

"Hey," Wyatt yelled up the passage.

"Hey," Relic replied, putting his face and headlamp into the shaft, blinding Wyatt. "Sorry," Relic said, diverting his light to the side. "You're almost home. There's another big cavern up here."

Sweeter words Wyatt could not imagine. He wiggled and pushed his way forward to the lip of the exit. There, Relic grabbed his hands and let Wyatt pull his head out into the open. Wyatt pushed against the side of the cliff, squirming his rear and legs the rest of the way out.

He flopped onto the ground like a fish in a boat and lay on his back, gasping.

Boom! An explosion reverberated through the rock like an earthquake, pounding from their ears all but its brute eruption, turning sound into a new kind of deafness.

"Back!" Relic yelled, reeling away from the passage.

Wyatt rolled toward Relic's feet and squatted next to him. The blast echoed again and again, fading slowly as it went.

"What the hell?" Wyatt asked.

"Must be Lynch. He shot up the tunnel, hoping he'd hit one of us."

"Shithead."

"Puss bucket. Asshole would have killed you in there."

"What do we do now?"

"Buy some time." Relic reached into his daypack and pulled out his Colt special. He walked over to the shaft, pointed it down the center and fired.

Boom! Buckshot bounced against the sides of the passage, shearing bits of stone and gravel into its depths, sending a fresh wave of echoes through the chamber.

"That ought to do it," Relic said.

"He'll think twice about coming up," Wyatt said. "But, we're trapped up here now."

"That's just the thing, there, Wyatt. Take a deep breath."

"I'm OK. I don't need to practice again."

"No, I mean smell the air."

Wyatt exhaled and then took that breath. He took another one. The dampness was gone. The stale smell of mud was gone. The air was cool and invigorating.

"That's right, man, take it all in. Fresh air. We might just have us a way outta here."

Chapter 39

Relic's headlamp flickered on and off as he led Wyatt across a level floor to the base of a pile of rocks maybe two stories high. He scanned the loose boulders for a route up, then turned off his light.

Wyatt left his penlight off, conserving what little may be left. His eyes slowly adjusted to the pitch black and were then pulled upward toward the top of the scree. There, just barely visible, was a diffuse stream of light.

"Oh my god," Wyatt said, "you've found a way out."

"Let's hope so." Relic turned his light back on and began to climb the unsteady blocks toward the top. Wyatt followed, veering off and back again to Relic's route as best he could.

Wyatt's hand slid off a loose rock and he skinned his elbow and cursed. He moved a few feet higher and a boulder the size of a stuffed suitcase slid from under his foot. He lay onto the rocks and pulled himself up, panting. Despite the fresh air, he was soon sweating again.

"Can you turn on your light again? Back here so I can see where I'm going." Wyatt asked.

Ten feet ahead, Relic switched on his head-lamp. He turned and lit the area in front of Wyatt.

"Thanks. Got it."

Relic turned the light in front of him for a moment then switched it off and resumed his climb.

Wyatt felt his way to a large boulder and scooted across to his left, then climbed farther up. Slowly, tips of the rock pile became visible from the outside light. He hurried his pace up the slope.

"Ow, shit," Relic said.

"What?"

"Low ceiling here. Shit."

Wyatt could see Relic rubbing his head, sil-houetted against the filtered sunlight. The rock pile angled steeply toward the roof of the cavern here, and the entrance seemed a lot narrower than the light flowing through it. He worked his way next to Relic and searched for an opening they could get through.

"Over here," Wyatt said, moving to his right. He came to a crooked vent about three feet wide and two feet tall. He pulled loose rock away from the opening and light flooded over him like a wave. He pushed himself through the crack and his head popped out atop a hill of dark rock. He wiggled the rest of the way out and crawled to the side.

He collapsed onto level dirt and stared into the dark blue sky, falling into deep space, an astronaut untethered from spaceship earth, spinning higher and higher into the ether. His head spun and his stomach too, until he had to close his eyes and grip the dusty ground with his fingers.

"Freedom," he heard Relic say.

Wyatt opened his eyes into narrow slits, letting them adjust to the light. Slowly, he regained his sense of balance and sat up. The hill they had climbed out of was much farther up the canyon than where they'd entered the cave. The layer of limestone seemed to dive back under the sand-stone about a quarter mile up, disappearing from the landscape entirely.

"No tellin' how many more caves there are under here, how far they go down into the bed-rock..." Relic said.

"We could have been in there forever," Wyatt said.

"Or for the rest of our lives." Relic nodded.

Chapter 40

Lynch shook his head to clear his mind. He could hardly believe those clowns had shot back at him through the cave. But he had them trapped now. He holstered his P4 and moved carefully back through the passage with the narrow ledge. Clinging to the rock wall, he shuffled his feet past the thin walkway. He was soon back in the chamber with the deep pool. He stepped carefully around it, to keep his boots dry, then scrambled over the boulders that led back to the man-made stairs. From there, he entered the large area where the entrance lay. He soon saw light from outside and squeezed through the crack where he'd had come in.

Cutter and Kowalski turned as they heard Lynch scrape against the rock. They pulled their pistols and held them at the ready.

"It's Lynch," Cutter said, re-holstering his weapon.

Lynch nodded.

Kowalski put his gun away and moved to Lynch's side.

"What's going on?" Kowalski asked.

Cutter worked his way closer to them.

"Two of them, the kid and his accomplice. I followed them in here, into the cave."

"Are they…?" Cutter asked.

"No. They crawled up a tunnel, and I couldn't get to them. I shot up at them, but I don't think I hit anyone. Then they fired a shot back at me, through the tunnel. But they're stuck in there. I looked all around and that cave only gets deeper. There's no way out, except right here." He pointed behind him.

"What do you want us to do?" Kowalski asked.

"Stay here. Cutter and I will go back to camp. Cutter will come back later and relieve you. He'll bring some water and food too."

Kowalski nodded.

"Got it," Cutter said.

"Guard the entrance. They've got a gun, so be careful. Don't take any chances. If you have to shoot them, you've got no problems from me," Lynch said.

Kowalski grinned.

****

"So they're trapped in the cave?" Winford asked. "You're sure this time?"

Lynch's face reddened, and he moved toward Winford.

Schmidt stepped between them. "No need to get huffy, Winford. You try chasing assholes in hundred-degree heat."

"Wyatt's a wimp," Winford said.

"The guy he's with is no wimp," Schmidt said. "He seems to know his way around these canyons like it's his own backyard."

Lynch turned from them and watched as workers moved in and out of the mess tent, a half-mile away.

"Damn it, how am I going to explain a missing associate?" Winford asked.

"He's been nothing but trouble, and now you want us to fix this?" Lynch turned back toward them.

"You should've had him in custody by now."

"You should never have brought an asshole like that along in the first place."

Schmidt looked at Winford, then Lynch. "Listen, guys, them hiding in this cave may make it easier. Your associate went off on a lark, a hike he was never up to doing. We looked everywhere. He probably died of dehydration somewhere. Maybe we even help the search party find the cave…eventually."

"There'll be search crews all over this place," Winford said.

"Sure. We'll be ready," Schmidt said. "How can the lenders fault us for some city boy who goes off half-cocked?"

"The certificate of completion…"

"I'll forge Wyatt's name. Get me some writing samples. We say he signed it before he went off into the desert," Schmidt said.

Winford scratched his chin and shifted his weight. "Could work..."

"Sure it'll work. Wyatt is trapped in that cave. He just solved the very problem he created..."

"Best news yet, dying in that cave will be no picnic." Lynch's lips tightened upward. "Unless they can get to water, they'll be dead by Thursday."

"Better send Cutter into the cave to guard the pool," Schmidt said.

"Right. No one searching the area will see him either, and he'll be cool and comfortable the whole time."

"Maybe I need to delay my departure by another day or so," Winford said tentatively.

"That's the spirit."

Chapter 41

Wyatt watched in silence as a blend of pink and orange rose along the far cliffs, icing the top with a sunset glaze. A pair of crows glided just below the rim, feathers dark and ragged-edged. Shadows had grown taller behind every rock and bush, filling the floor of the small canyon with stripes of black and gold.

They'd sat there for a long time, sipping on Relic's water bottle, thinking about the cave, feeling the joy of its release, saying not a word. Wyatt's heart finally found a natural pace, his skin cooled by the evening breeze. He shifted his legs.

"After being trapped in that cave, this place seems...supernatural," Wyatt said. "All the colors, the shapes, how it's all spread out in front of us." The cliff face changed its expression as a crescent of sunset lit the upper rim.

"Supernatural? Yes, that's an interesting way to say it." Relic watched the far side of the canyon. "My grandfather told me even the rocks have their own life, a spiritual side to them."

Wyatt had never heard that before, but right now, in this time and place, the idea seemed entirely self-evident. He took a deep breath of the evening air and something about his location in the universe seemed to shift. He stared at the shadows of crows as they dashed across the upper cliffs and felt the rhythm of his own pulse.

"Hate to go, but we best move along and make a quick camp," Relic said.

"What about Lynch, back in the cave?" Wyatt asked.

"That man has his own troubles," Relic said.

"He's not dumb though."

"He couldn't pour piss from a boot."

Wyatt figured Relic meant that they shared a low opinion of Lynch.

"I wonder if he followed us up. Or maybe he turned around at that passageway."

"Thinking about the inner tube?" Relic smiled.

"Yeah, that one. The pneumatic tube," Wyatt said with a sense of awe.

"The Hopi say we emerged through an underworld into this one, the fourth world…"

"Fourth world?"

"Three before this one, for all of mankind."

"Really."

"Gettin' loose of that crawlspace has me thinking about that…gettin' loose of one world and into the next," Relic said.

Wyatt let his mind wander around the thought. "The crawlspace was bad enough, but the headspace is what just about ended it for me." He turned away from Relic to hide the tears that were filling his eyes. "I found out how much I love the open air."

Relic patted Wyatt's shoulder, then his smile, tight and grim at first, melted into something joyous.

"Well, we've got to find a place to camp for the night. I remember a little sheltered spot across the flats, to the west. Along the cliffs down there a bit." He motioned to the south.

"Do you know every nook and cranny in this country?"

"Some say."

"Well, how far? I'm beat."

"Not bad, maybe a mile from here. We'd best get across the way while there's light."

"Slave driver," Wyatt said, but with some humor. "You assume my joints will bend." He stood slowly and rested his hands on his knees for a moment.

Relic rose slowly too, and stretched.

Wyatt walked back to their exit from the cave and listened, then peered inside. Nothing. Relic began a casual stride down the side of the hillock, weaving around loose rock and a patch of prickly pear cactus. Wyatt turned and forced one foot in front of the other. At least it's downhill, he thought.

They finished coming downslope and the ground leveled out in front of them. The sandy earth had more clumps of grass here than in the main canyon lower down, and less sage. Several scrub oak dotted the far side of the plain at the

base of the high cliffs. Daylight was fading. Colors
became pale and ashen, blending into shadows of
charcoal and soot.

They walked for nearly a mile across, Wyatt
too tired to speak. When he thought his legs would
give out for certain, Relic motioned them toward
a drop along the canyon floor, to a spot where a
lone cedar met the wall of sandstone. About twenty
yards beyond that was a gentle overhang of cliff.

Relic moved to the bottom of the shallow
shelter, sat cross-legged, and removed his daypack.
He pulled his hair from its pony tail and combed
it with his fingers, looking much younger in the
semi-dark, a twenty-year-old with wisps of silver
in his mane. He took out the bladder of water from
his pack and poured it carefully into the water
bottle until it was full again. He lifted the rubber
container, showing Wyatt it was still two thirds
full.

Wyatt plodded toward Relic and nearly fell to
the ground next to him.

"Drink."

Wyatt rolled himself to a sitting position and
rested his back on the cliff wall. He took the bottle
and drank.

By the time Relic had a little fire going, the
night sky was black as pitch. Relic poked the young
blaze with a stick. Wyatt lay back on the sand.
Glowing ashes stirred into the air and blended
with the sparks of distant stars, the fever of what
was near at hand as hot and real as the suns a million miles away.

"Want some supper?"

Wyatt was asleep before he could answer.

Chapter 42

Wyatt woke to the sound of twisting metal. He rolled from his fetal position onto one elbow and looked around.

"Mornin'," Relic said.

"Hmph."

"Got a real treat for us for breakfast today." Relic peeled the lid of a can back against itself with part of a small can opener. "Here." He set the tin next to Wyatt, balanced a tortilla on top, and rummaged through his pack. He pulled out another can of pineapple chunks and began to open it too.

Wyatt sat up slowly. Every muscle ached with movement, tightened against his joints like a rubber band with rigor mortis.

Relic grabbed his own tortilla, rolled it up, and dipped it into the pineapple juice. He pulled it out and bit off the soaked end while he pulled a wicked looking knife from his pocket. He swallowed, then drove the knife into the can and fished out a chunk of pineapple. Dribbles of the juice ran down his thin goatee and dropped into the sand at his bare feet.

Wyatt dipped and ate the tortilla then took a swig of the sweet juice and rolled it around his mouth.

Relic released a short belch, announcing his completion of the meal. He handed his knife to Wyatt.

"Have you been carrying these cans around all this time?" Wyatt asked, spearing a pineapple.

"Sure. Got 'em at the commissary."

"The mess tent?"

"Where else?"

Wyatt ate steadily, alternating between the juice-soaked tortilla and chunks of fruit. When he was done, he put the knife in the empty can and placed it closer to Relic.

"Better take your shoes off for a while, let your feet air out."

Wyatt removed his shoes, battered and torn along the outer edges. Probably where he scraped his way through the inner tube, he thought. He pulled his socks off and got a whiff of what smelled like raw sewage bubbling up the pipes in his high school gym. After a wrestling match. As his nose recovered, he massaged his toes and popped their knuckles.

Relic reorganized his pack, putting the trash in an outer pocket. He took a pull on his water and handed the bottle to Wyatt.

"Leave us half a bottle."

Wyatt nodded. "What's next?"

"We gotta get more water, for sure. Best place

to get it now is probably the river or at your camp."

"I keep telling you, it's not my camp."

"Sorry. Right. We can go back to their camp, or swing south and avoid the crowd."

"Lynch is ready to kill us," Wyatt said. "Literally."

"Sure as sunrise," Relic nodded.

"I need to get back to a town, someplace, where I can call the firm and tell them what's been going on. And call law enforcement."

"Wyatt." Relic shook his head. "I can't tell you what to do. But listen to me before you decide. Your boss didn't get where he is today without support from your firm. His partners are just like he is, or maybe they tolerate him because he makes them a mint. They are not going to believe you over him."

"They'll have to. I'll tell them everything that happened. Hell, I can show them if I need to."

"Look. You can be a real turd-snapper when you want to…"

"What…"

"But you're not a bad guy down deep."

"Wow. Thanks," Wyatt said with a hint of sarcasm.

"You're welcome," Relic smiled.

"What choice do I have? I have to go back home eventually, try to get my job back."

"Someone once said we all have our 'yes' and we all have our 'no.' Most of the time, I think that's all we have. Everybody has a choice, we just talk ourselves out of making the best ones half the time. Usually 'cause they're hard. But do you really want to go back to work for those guys? Do you really think you have no choices left?"

"I'm not like you. I can't live like this," Wyatt spread his hands.

"You've been living like this for days now," Relic let a corner of his mouth lift into a crooked grin.

"With your help, we survived, somehow."

"Do you think what your boss is doing in these canyons is wrong?"

"Yes, absolutely."

"Want to help me stop him?"

Wyatt's eyebrow rose.

Chapter 43

"Help you how?" Wyatt asked.

Relic began putting his socks and boots on. "We're going back down to the lower canyon for water. And re-provisions."

"Then what?" Wyatt put his socks on too.

"Time to toss a monkey into the works. Let me think some more, and by the time we're there, I'll lay it out for us."

"If I don't like the plan?" He pulled on his shoes and laced them.

"You can head back up the new road these jackasses have plowed, walk back to a 'town' as you call it, and beg for help. Or, you can stick with me a little while longer and we can fight back against these thieves." Relic stood up and shouldered his pack.

Wyatt pushed himself up against the cliff and worked into an upright position. Something told him Relic's plan was not going to be easy.

"Your muscles will loosen up with the walk,

and it will give us both time to think things through."

Wyatt took a deep breath and followed Relic out into the open grasses. They moved slowly at first, scanning the field and the hill on the other side, where they'd left the cave the day before, watching for Lynch. Relic took a winding route roughly parallel with the nearest cliffs. The canyon sloped gently downward for a long while, and they reached a tumble of boulders leading more steeply toward the main canyon. They wandered at an easy pace around rocks the size of trailers, lowering themselves carefully in places between them.

Conversations he'd had with Winford rolled through Wyatt's mind. "Come with me," Winford would say in his haughty tone. "You'll do," he'd say when he wanted someone else to perform a task but Wyatt was the one available. What had he ever done wrong? Was he lousy at his job? Insubordinate? An asshole?

No. He knew every sentence from every witness, every document relevant to every proceeding. He busted his ass, but Winford was inherently superior to everyone. That was Winford's whole approach to the world. Why did that make Wyatt want to please him all the more? So he could attain the same position as Winford someday? So he could become another Winford? It was the only thing that made sense, and he felt his stomach wrench.

He stopped at the top of a boulder, walked out to the edge of it, and sat. Relic kept a steady pace ahead of him, but Wyatt was not too worried about catching up. This area seemed to be safe. He recognized the flats far to his right and the wall of sandstone above it. That was where he and Relic had come the day before, or was it the day before that? He could see where the arroyo should be, hidden from view, along the base of the towering stone. The cliffs seemed to dwarf everything else on the planet. For a change, he knew right where he was.

When someone is a hostage, Wyatt thought, he sometimes adopts the goals of his captor just to survive, or even to find a way to thrive. Unfair treatment is ignored, or even welcomed if the victim accepts the idea that he is inferior to the master. A hostage and a kidnapper. A sick relation-ship, but a survival mechanism. Was it possible to be in that kind of syndrome working for someone like Todd Winford the Fourth? Now it seemed not only possible, but highly likely.

Relic turned, gave him a quick wave, and found a place to rest.

Wyatt thought again about being stuck in the "inner tube," his breath cut in half, his body frozen in place, his mind panicked and ripe for torture, a morsel for the devil himself. But he'd gotten out of there.

Chapter 44

Relic stood below him, pointing to an area that Wyatt assumed was the easiest way down. Wyatt stretched his legs, walked away from the edge of the rock he'd been sitting on, and climbed down a tangle of stone. Maybe twelve feet lower, he stepped through some loose rock to a patch of level ground. He followed that around to where Relic waited.

"I want to take us over there." Relic stretched his arm to the north. "There are two ridges that reach into the main canyon and end above, and some distance from, the work camp. Like two fingers reaching into the flats. I was on the northern ridge, which we will be on if we keep going straight, when I saw Lynch shoot that man in the chest." He pointed to their right.

"You saw them from here?" Wyatt asked.

"From farther down, yes." Relic put his hands on his hips and stared at the landscape. "You need to check this out." He began his easy lope across the ground and Wyatt hurried to keep up.

There was no trail to follow and it took them nearly an hour to reach where the northern and southern ridges split. From there, they crossed open sandstone to the northern ridge and made their way west. The area was remarkably remote and well hidden. They moved hastily along the northern ridge until they reached a high sandstone bowl. They eased carefully down to the next level, jumping a few feet to the bottom. Going back up this way could be difficult.

They continued along the lower level of the ridge another half-mile until they reached a clearing. A panel of flat, mahogany colored sandstone rose about twenty feet from the sandy bottom.

Relic looked across the chasm to the southern ridge, then back at the low cliffs. He moved along carefully, glancing back and forth until he seemed satisfied.

"Along in here, I'm pretty sure," Relic said.

Wyatt followed, examining the ground as he walked.

"Shit on a shingle." Relic stopped suddenly.

There, right in front of them, stood two petroglyph warriors stationed below, if they believed their eyes, the yawning jaws and naked skull of a meat-eating dinosaur.

Chapter 45

"Whoa. I've never seen petroglyphs anything like this." Wyatt waved his hand at the panel. Beside the large carnivore skull were the shapes of whole animals, like lizards, some standing on two feet, some on four, and one with the distinctive neck and tail of an herbivore, maybe a brontosaurus. The thunder lizard himself.

"Me neither." Relic leaned close to the rock, examining the pecks and scratches of sandstone that outlined the teeth of an ancient raptor. "Impeccable work." He ran his finger along the rock art, not quite touching it.

"Did the old ones do any of these anywhere else?" Wyatt asked.

"Thing is, the old ones didn't do these. Well, not all of them."

"What? They sure look real to me. Look at how worn it is along the edges."

"The wear looks right over all, sure enough, but I've been here before…"

"What?"

"The two warriors there, toward the bottom, are real."

"None of the dinosaurs are real?"

"Well, to be honest, one of them is real."

"One? Which one?"

Relic turned toward Wyatt. "It's our secret that one of these is the real deal. Right?"

"OK, yes, sure. Why?"

"If anyone else knew there was a real one among the fakes, this place would be trampled and studied to death. Every tabloid would be camped out here, making a living talking about it. Every tourist in the country would want to see it."

"It would wreck this whole area," Wyatt said softly.

"Indeed."

"Just like his Lord Winnieship is doing."

"Exactly."

"Promise me."

"I promise." Wyatt thought for a moment and shook his head. "Wait. No. I don't need to know which one. I shouldn't know which one."

"Someday, we'll come back here, you and me."

Wyatt looked up.

"And I'll show you then."

Wyatt straightened. "Raptor Canyon, LLC. That's what Winford and his partners are calling this project. I assumed it had something to do with falcons or maybe fossils…"

"There's a fossil bed about five miles from here, too remote to reach except by foot or horseback," Relic said.

"But it's all about these petroglyphs. It was Winford's plan from the beginning," Wyatt pointed at the dinosaur skull, "or he wouldn't have named it Raptor Canyon. He's going to cash in on this."

"Why get an artist to carve a whole panel of fake dinosaurs when you have a real one here already?" Relic asked.

"No, see, it fits Winford's personality. He wants a cash cow, he needs a sensational site. The way he thinks, one petroglyph would never be enough."

Relic rubbed his forehead.

Wyatt looked into the distance. "I wonder if the blond man told them one of the dinosaur petros was real…"

"Maybe he found it on his own and decided this was the natural place to add his new petros. If he hadn't found it up here, it woulda been easier to carve his own art lower in the canyon. And better to put it closer to the resort," Relic said.

"Yeah."

"He said 'treasure,' before he died. 'Treasure' and 'hoax.'"

"The treasure is the real dinosaur petroglyph," Wyatt said. "Right?"

"Must be. But who set up a hoax on who?"

"We may never know for sure," Wyatt said.

Relic removed his pack and found his binoculars. He walked to a flat, sandy area at the base of the sandstone and wandered around, eyes on the ground. Then he searched the other ridge with his binoculars and up and down the shallow canyon in between.

Wyatt stepped back from the petroglyph for a better view of its placement on the rock. "So, why would Lynch kill the artist up here?"

"It's remote…" Relic said, turning back toward Wyatt.

"There's plenty of remote places in this canyon…"

"These dino petros are what got him shot," Relic said, frowning. "Real or not, these petros are part of a very dangerous plan to make some very serious people rich."

"Jurassic Park."

"Except the killers aren't dinosaurs." Relic looked toward the southern ridge, the direction of the distant camp.

Wyatt took a deep breath. He hadn't exactly disbelieved Relic about the shooting that happened here, but now it was concrete, a real place, a real death. Lynch killed him because he knew the rock art was a fake. The artist could prove it. And Lynch must have moved the body, because there was nothing here but these stunning petroglyphs. Had he buried the man nearby?

About the size of a large living room, the area in front of the rock art looked like it had been cleared of brush and grass and maybe even leveled. Wyatt found a trail at the end opposite from where they'd come.

"I want to see where this leads," Wyatt pointed.

Relic nodded and followed. The path was lined with brush but was well worn. A quarter of a mile down the winding trail, they came to the top of a huge, rounded block of sandstone, about thirty yards across. To their left rose a set of wooden stairs, the pine still sharp-edged and fresh. Without it, access would be difficult, Wyatt thought. You would need climbing ropes or ladders to get up here from below.

The valley opened wide before them, glowing under the mid-day sun. The northern cliffs rose a thousand feet above the canyon floor far to their right, above where he and Relic had run up the arroyo. The ridge they were on extended to the south another fifty yards or so, hiding the work camp from view. Below, the trail resumed at the foot of the stairs, winding around the rocky point and then out of sight.

"Let's sit over here," Relic motioned. Wyatt followed him to a shaded overhang at the top of the giant sandstone block.

"Drink?" Wyatt asked.

Relic handed him the bottle, put the binoculars to his eyes again, and scanned the flats.

"The rest is yours," Wyatt said. Relic took the bottle and finished it dry. He pulled the bladder from his pack and refilled the bottle. Only about four inches of water was left in the soft plastic container.

"We're OK for a few hours, but in this heat, we're going to need water again soon." He pulled his pack off and put the binoculars away.

"What do you think we should do?" Wyatt asked.

"Rest."

"No, I mean, what are we going to do about

all of this?" Wyatt waved his hand back toward the petroglyphs.

"I've got a rough plan," Relic said.

"I'm your man."

Relic took a breath. "Don't take this wrong, Wyatt, but you should be your own man…Be sure you don't replace Lord Winnieship down there with me, or anybody else. Be sure you're making your own path."

Wyatt's face flushed for a moment and he cleared his throat.

"Join me as a friend, if you like, not as a… subordinate. That's all I mean." Relic's dark eyes shined.

"That's exactly what I want to do."

"Then let me tell you what I have in mind…" Relic smoothed the dust in front of their feet and began to map it out.

Chapter 46

After their talk, Wyatt had lain back on the smooth sandstone and fallen asleep immediately. Relic did not need to repeat his suggestion for a nap.

What woke him now was unclear – maybe it was an evening breeze or a stirring from Relic, who slept a few feet away. He rolled onto his side and then sat up, resting his arms on his knees. Before him rose the northernmost cliff, its personality changing with each degree of movement from the sun. At mid-day, the mud-brown stone had stared impassively across the canyon, baking the earth. Now, its amber skin had cooled and shadows moved like desert tortoises, revealing countless expressions, the crags and wrinkles in an old man's face.

Wyatt slid his rear out farther on the ledge and he looked to the west. Beyond the cottonwood trees by the river rose layers of rim after rim, ragged like torn paper, each one hazier in the distance until they disappeared.

Wyatt sensed movement and looked behind him. Relic sat cross-legged, his face to the west, eyes closed. His smile carried a sense of deep satisfaction, like a yogi in meditation. Wyatt turned back to the sun and watched it disappear into the curve of the planet.

"Ready?" Relic asked.

"Yes." Wyatt stood and brushed off his pants. He moved around the rocks they'd used for shade and examined the top of the long sandstone block and the wooden stairs that leaned against it. All was empty. Below, along the trail, two does walked gingerly in the light of dusk, raising their legs in dainty steps. He walked across the rock to the wooden railing and tested its strength. The beams were heavy and bolted, not nailed, together. It was built to take some heavy traffic.

He started down the stairs, listening to Relic shuffle behind him. He felt exposed here, out in the open, on Lynch's turf. He waited for a moment at the bottom, then walked along the trail where the deer had gone. Relic followed and they both cleared the corner.

Canvas tents rested in the distance in uneven rows, their entrance peaks white like the waves atop the rapids. A blue truck the size of a matchbox bounced its way north through the canyon, rotating a searchlight in the dusk. Lynch's men. Wyatt and Relic stayed east of the tent city until they neared the other side, then made their way quietly, but openly, toward the mess tent. The dinner meal should be finished, the kitchen crew cleaning up. Construction workers and heavy equipment operators would be tired, back in their tents, or maybe playing poker in the dining room. If they were lucky, they could get some late food and replenish their water before starting the task at hand. Wyatt's heart jumped a beat as he thought about walking straight into the sanctuary of men like Winford, Schmidt, and Lynch.

A group of men made their way toward the open mess, talking among themselves, some carrying jackets. Relic slipped off his pack and carried it in his right hand. Relic and Wyatt folded in behind the workers and kept their eyes cast to the ground. A man in a yellow "Security" t-shirt stood just inside the entrance, his arms crossed, his eyes scanning the group as they entered. Lynch would have his team looking for them. But they passed quickly and without notice, separating from each other and working their way to a large table with everyone else. Relic peeled away and went to the kitchen entrance, stepping behind the portable dividers and out of sight from the sentry. Wyatt held back, glancing toward the guy in the yellow t-shirt, then quickly walking to the same entrance.

"Kitchen's closed," a woman's voice boomed. She stood by the grill, her back to Relic and Wyatt.

"Just need to refill my water," Relic said.

"Drinking water's outside the tent." She twisted around to see them. "You know that."

"But I'm in here..." Relic held out his water bottle and gave her his warmest smile.

"Wait. You..." She set a wire brush on top of the grill and wiped her hands on her apron. She had deep-set brown eyes with a no-nonsense look about her. She tucked a loose strand of hair behind her ear and her expression softened.

"You can't be comin' back here again. I helped your poor soul the first time, the second time's a sin."

"I'm not here for a handout. I'll clean that grill so hard you'll have to sweep up the metal shavings when I'm done." Relic pointed behind her. "Fair trade?"

"Who's this sorry ass you dragged in here with you?" She pointed at Wyatt.

"Oh, he actually works here, ma'am, I just happened to run into him on the way in here.

"Oh, really?" She looked at Wyatt from head to toe, sizing up a cut of meat.

"That's right," Wyatt said.

"Don't bullshit me," she said, turning toward the portable coolers. "If either of you want something from my kitchen at this late hour, you have to earn it."

"Yes, ma'am." Relic set his pack by the table. He picked up a cleaning pad, then moved to the grill and began scrubbing it. He motioned for Wyatt to help.

"Clean those filthy hands before you work on my grill."

Relic seemed to be enjoying himself, smiling like he was in a Fourth of July Parade. "Yes, ma'am." They scrubbed up at the sink, stoppered it, filled it with hot soapy water, and began scouring the grill. The woman in charge sat on a stool and watched them like a falcon.

"You missed a spot," Relic said to Wyatt with a wink.

Wyatt splashed a little more than he had to and rubbed the steel wool even harder against the blackened grill. "What's up with you?" Wyatt whispered. "Looking for a date?"

"Be nice. She's a kind soul, that's all, and she's funny as hell."

"You must be starved for humor."

"Yeah. Been hangin' around you too long."

Chapter 47

"All right, you two, finish up over there, then help yourself. There's fresh stew in the silver pots in the fridge, still mostly warm. Bread on the top shelf to your right. You can refill your water at the sink…" She smiled and slid off her stool. "I'm too tired not to trust you, so mind your manners. Another fourteen-hour day, and I'm done in." She waved absentmindedly in their direction and left the kitchen.

"Let's finish up so we can put the grill back together," Relic said.

Wyatt looked at him, his question implicit.

"Matter of honor, is all."

They scrubbed and rinsed and put it all back where it belonged. Relic filled his water bottle, then removed the rubber bladder from his pack and filled it too. Wyatt found two bowls and pulled the stew from the cooler. He pulled half a loaf of French bread from the shelf and found spoons. They could hear bits of conversation on the other side of the dividers, some in English, some in Spanish, men visiting after a hard day's work.

Wyatt poured the stew and began eating. Warm enough. He tore off a piece of bread and ate at a steady pace. Relic seemed to be re-organizing his pack, then went to the cupboards. He pulled two cans of pears and put them in the bottom of his pack and filled the rest of the space with more jerky, tortillas, and M&Ms.

When Wyatt had had his fill, Relic poured himself some stew and drank it from the bowl. "See if you can find toothpicks," he said under his breath. "A couple of boxes. And glue."

"Toothpicks?" Wyatt whispered to himself. He searched the shelves and spotted two boxes.

"And sugar," Relic said. "See if there's something we can carry it in, a bag or a box..."

Wyatt searched under the sink and found two empty white buckets with handles. He found flour and sugar on an upper shelf. He put three five-pound bags of sugar into each bucket, two upright, one sideways on top. Then he put black plastic trash bags over the sugar, to hide them.

"Are we going out the front with these?" Wyatt asked.

Relic looked around. "Let's make an exit in the back, behind the food trays."

"Need anything else?"

"Find some glue?"

"Not yet."

"I think we've pushed our luck far enough," Relic said. "Let's skedaddle."

Relic shouldered his pack and pulled out his

hunting knife. They went behind an aluminum stack used for storing trays and huddled behind it. Relic stabbed the tent and worked his blade down to the floor. He pulled it apart, bent down, and went through, Wyatt right behind him. Wyatt stood up outside and turned around, a bucket in each hand.

"Stop right there," she said, a serrated steak knife three inches from Wyatt's neck.

Chapter 48

Wyatt dropped the buckets reflexively. The loud chunk made his face twitch, and he jumped and shivered with tension, holding his ground, unsure what to expect. Then, Wyatt took a subtle step backward and saw Relic to his right, hands in the air. Wyatt raised his palms slowly and watched as the woman's shadowed face turned from Relic to Wyatt and back.

"What are you doing here?" she asked.

They stood in silence for several moments. Wyatt could hear the generator running on the far side of the tent. Lights hung haphazardly on poles around the mess tent, coating the ground with a jaundiced glow. They must have come on while he and Relic were inside.

"I work here," Wyatt began.

She narrowed her eyes in disbelief.

"Not on the crew," he added quickly. "I work for Winnie, shit, Winford, one of the partners on the project. I'm a lawyer."

"A lawyer. Stealing buckets from the mess tent in the middle of the night." She stepped back and shadows lifted from her like a curtain. She was the girl who had startled him days ago, in the mess tent, when Lynch was brandishing a pistol at him and Relic. The one whose expression had so surprised him. She wore a blue smock of sorts, her near-black hair in a tight bun and food servers net. She lowered her knife a few inches and put her left fist on her hip. Dark chocolate eyes peered skeptically from under her brow.

"While you're in the mood for tall tales, I want to hear his story too." She pointed the knife at Relic. "You look familiar to me. Weren't you in here a few days ago?"

"We're harmless, miss, really," Wyatt said.

"Why not go back out the entrance, where the security guard is?" she asked pointedly.

"Well, shit. Tell her, Relic."

"Relic?" she asked.

"That's him." Wyatt nodded in Relic's direction. "It's an unusual name, I'll grant you that."

Relic kept his palms up, but lowered them to his shoulders. "Wait, I know you… Faye?"

Her eyes narrowed and she moved the blade toward his stomach.

"Knew your grandpa too, when he was alive."

"Move over," she motioned at Relic with the knife, "into better light." He slid to his left. She moved closer, examining his face.

"Crap!" She stepped back. "Relic?"

He smiled and nodded.

"You knew my grandpa. You used to pal

around with him when I was a kid, right?"

"Yes."

"Wait. What was my grandpa's name?"

"Cal Snow. But we all called him Old Man Snow."

"It is you!" She lowered her knife and gave Relic a giant hug. He put his arms around her. "Here," she said, locking her arm in his, swinging the scalloped blade about like a harmless twig, "let's blow this popsicle stand." She proceeded to lead Relic away from the mess tent and out of the lights.

Wyatt put his arms down.

"He's with you?" she asked Relic.

"Yep."

"A lawyer?"

"I've learned to tolerate him." Relic turned and winked at Wyatt. "Don't forget the buckets," he called back after them.

Wyatt couldn't quite hear him.

Chapter 49

Wyatt followed their voices and shadows until they were all far away from the mess tent. They wound their way along a narrow path toward the sound of the gurgling river. The final glow of sunset faded in the distance, replaced with a scattering of stars and the diffused light of camp. The trail led past a cottonwood then down an embankment to a sandy spot several yards from the water. A small backpacker's tent was pitched near a fire ring. Relic and Faye sat in the sand together. Wyatt sat next to Relic.

"Let me get a fire going," she said, reaching for sticks and placing them along the rocks. She lit a handful of grass under the twigs and blew gently, encouraging it. She broke a larger branch in two, laid them over the young flame, and sat back.

"So, you knew her grandfather?" Wyatt asked Relic.

"Yep. He owned the ranch south and west of here. Died about a year ago." Relic tossed another stick on the fire.

"Year and a half," Faye corrected.

"Somehow, well…did you lose this corner of the ranch?" Relic asked.

Her mouth hardened. "Not lost. Stole." She shook her head angrily. "We had a good lawyer, but he died or retired a few years ago. Sold his practice to a big firm out of Denver. Grandpa thought he needed money for the ranch while my sister and I were off at college. When we got back, he told us he'd gotten into a partnership with a company that wanted to invest in ranching in Little Horse Canyon, so they called the company that. We didn't think too much about it until he passed away. That's when we read the agreement. Said the partners inherited his share of the company. The company owns this piece of the land here, a triangle-shaped parcel on the far edge of the ranch. But as you can see, it's a beautiful, pristine canyon."

"Or, it was," Relic whispered.

"Yeah," she agreed.

"What did you do?" Wyatt asked.

"I was madder than a wet hen. Grandpa never would have let any part of this ranch go outside the family. He'd been swindled. And it was a smart con too. A slow one, one that no one could undo after he died."

"I didn't think anyone could con Snow," Relic said.

"His final years were good to him, physically, and I really hate to say this, but his memory was going. He worried about us girls, and, like all of us, he worried about money. He got it in his head that he had to get investors to help us out. But he was confused. When he told us about the deal, he said our old lawyer put it together, but it turned out it was this new guy, this Winford guy."

His Lord Winnieship, Wyatt thought.

"He's crooked as a dog's hind leg," Relic said, patting Faye on the shoulder. "There wasn't much Snow or anyone else could have done, except steer clear of him."

"That's why you're out here," Wyatt said flatly. "Checking the work being done here, checking the project."

"I'm not making much progress though. Signed on as kitchen help to see what's up. I know where they're going to build the lodge and that they don't call it Little Horse Canyon anymore."

"Winford probably formed another corporation and bought it out, to add a couple layers of liability protection. Now it's called Raptor Canyon," Wyatt said.

"After the falcons that nest here?" she asked.

"Not exactly…" Wyatt glanced at Relic.

"But you know about the project…" Faye leaned forward.

"Parts of it. I had no idea Winford was one of the partners until I came out here with him. There's a guy named Lynch," Wyatt and Relic looked at each other, "who's one of the partners. Another guy named Schmidt is the third one. They all own the company, which owns the canyon."

"And they're developing the shit out of it," Faye said.

"That's not the half of it," Relic tossed another

stick onto the fire.

Chapter 50

Relic explained that Lynch had chased them up the arroyo that ran along the northern cliffs, then east, into a higher canyon. Faye listened intently, nodding as he went along.

And, there's a really, uh…" Relic looked at Wyatt for a moment.

"unusual…"

Relic nodded, "... unusual set of petroglyphs on the north ridge. Faye, one is the skull of a dinosaur, like a small Tyrannosaurus, a raptor of some kind."

"Sheee-it." She sounded like a cowpoke. "There's been a lot of talk the last few years about the possibility of the ancient ones drawing dinosaurs," Faye said, gazing into the fire. "There's some dino track petros down on the Navajo Reservation, they say."

"Well, Winford's got himself a real, live, full-blown dinosaur petroglyph panel right here," Wyatt said.

"If it's real." Faye raised her brow.

"Real enough to get somebody shot," Wyatt said.

"Don't matter," Relic shook his head. "Real or not, it's his tourist attraction. He's built a staircase up the cliff to get to the damn thing."

"Stairs?"

"Yep."

"He's going to turn this little corner of paradise into Crappyland," she said.

"Winford and his partners have a loan agreement." Wyatt crossed his legs. "They've financed all of this, so far, by themselves. But they get ten million dollars once they complete the first phase on their own. I'm supposed to fill out the certificate of completion for this phase this week."

She held her palm toward him, as if to say, "what about that?"

"No chance he'll ask me to do it now. He'll find somebody else to sign it."

"So, they finish phase one, they get their money? And keep on building?"

"That's about the size of it." Relic pulled a plastic flask from a side pocket in his pack and passed it to Wyatt.

Wyatt opened, smelled quickly, and tossed a shot down his throat. "Aggg."

Relic took the flask and handed it to Faye.

"Homemade?"

"Sure."

She took a drink and coughed. "I forgot you knew how to make this poison."

"Your granddaddy didn't think it was too

bad." He smiled. "Wyatt, hand me the toothpicks."

Wyatt pulled them from his pockets and set them in front of Relic.

"Oh, no," Faye said.

"What the hell are these for?" Wyatt asked.

"To topple the empire," Relic announced.

"I know what you're planning." Faye gave Relic a sly grin, then looked to Wyatt. "You jam them into anything around here with a lock on it. Freezes them up. They have to pry their shit open or bring in a locksmith. That's it, isn't it Relic? A little monkey wrenching?"

"How do you know how to do this?" Wyatt asked.

"Gandhi. Peaceful resistance. Use the enemy's own practices against them," Relic said.

"No shit."

"You should know this, Wyatt. Like you, Gandhi was a lawyer."

"No shit."

"Tactical judo."

"No shit."

"Quit with the 'no shit,' would you?" Faye's eyes sparkled in the firelight. "I prefer Ed Abbey, anyway."

Relic grinned. "We need to hit the heavy equipment and trucks."

"Sugar for the gas tanks?" Faye asked.

"Crap."

"What?"

"Sugar's back at the tent, where I dropped it," Wyatt said.

"Some for the tanks, some for my still, but no

worries," Relic shrugged.

"There's a motor pool, of sorts, down river from here," Faye said. "They have what looks like a 500-gallon tank for fuel, and a mechanic. They tend to park the trucks there at night, so they can gas up for each day."

"What about the security guys?" Relic asked.

"There's a bunch of them, I counted three who wear the 'Security' t-shirts, not including the one who chased you all over the place," Faye said.

"Do they patrol in a regular pattern?"

She thought for a moment. "Yeah, I've been watching them. They go clockwise, starting from the mess tent area. They all have those heavy flashlights, the ones that double as billy clubs."

"Guns?"

"Probably."

"Here's what we do. We stick together at first and find a security patrol. We hang back from them, but follow them on their rounds, jamming their locks shut behind them. We can see them by their flashlights."

"Two boxes of toothpicks to take on Todd Winford the Fourth?" Wyatt asked.

"I've got some ideas too," Faye's eyes glittered. "I won't need the toothpicks, I've got bolt cutters. I'll start with you guys, then peel off."

"Uh-oh," Relic smiled and passed his flask to Wyatt again. "If you're gonna risk getting busted, losing your job, maybe your career, you'd better have a few more belts in you."

Faye's expression deepened. "I didn't think about that. You don't have to do this, Wyatt."

He took a deep drink of homemade gin, grimaced, then handed the liquor back to Relic. "Yes, actually, I'm pretty sure I do." He smiled.

Chapter 51

They gathered their things and followed Faye
away from the river bed and onto the level plain.
Voices floated toward them from the mess tent,
jumbles of words punctuated with laughter. As
they walked to the north, they saw a sword of light
crisscrossing the ground, lighting trucks and metal
drums and stacks of metal scraps with a dizzy
speed.

Relic motioned for Wyatt to follow him to
a pickup truck to their left. He lit his headlamp
briefly, shielding it from the security guard ahead
of them. He shook out a toothpick and slid it into
the keyhole on the passenger side. When it would
go no farther, he pulled it back out a bit, broke off
the end, and used the broken piece to push the rest
of it into the lock. He repeated the process with
more toothpicks. Nothing stuck out of the door
handle when he was done. Wyatt watched carefully
as Relic repeated the process on the driver's side.

"Got it?" Relic asked.

"Easy," Wyatt answered.

"A pebble in the tire valve will let the air out," Relic said.

"There's a bulldozer on the right," Faye whispered. "But leave that one to me. Catch up with you guys later."

"Let's try to meet at the base of the wooden stairs," Relic said. "If conditions allow."

"Sure." Faye nodded.

"And, listen, there's no reason to get caught if we don't have to. Keep moving. Improvise when you can, but getting away is a good thing, right?" Relic said.

"Right," Faye and Wyatt answered together. "Nothing wrong with a getaway," she added, patting Wyatt on the shoulder. "See you later." Faye turned and trotted out of sight.

The guard's roving light continued to move through a row of parked trucks and four-wheelers about forty yards ahead. Relic moved to a truck on their left, Wyatt to one on their right. They worked through a series of six other trucks, Relic using his headlamp when he needed to, Wyatt his penlight. For once, Wyatt was glad the light was weak – it would be harder for the guard to notice.

Wyatt saw a large backhoe to his right and searched the area for Relic. He knelt by the front tire of a pickup and listened carefully. Having finished his check at the motor pool, the guard seemed to be walking more directly north, quickly getting farther away.

****

Faye walked boldly to the mess tent entrance and went inside. She went along the side to a storage area and grabbed a broom, then turned and moved to the front again. There, she swept the wooden floor in front of the giant tent, looking casually to her left and right. Two men leaned unsteadily on a light pole, passing a bottle between them. Liquor was technically prohibited in the camp, but many of the workers smuggled it in. Faye kept a few beers hidden in the middle refrigerator, behind the eggs. The days were long, hot, and tough, and most men were away from their families for a week at a time. A couple of shots took the edge off.

No one seemed to notice her. She kept the broom in her hand and walked out of the light, toward the bulldozer. There, she moved quickly to gather a heavy chain nearby. She looped the chain around her right arm and shuffled quietly back, laying it on the ground in a straight line as she went. When she reached the edge of the lights, she looked around again and moved forward.

A man shouted, "Damn, you're a lucky sonofagun!" He stumbled out of the tent. Five or six others crowded at the entrance, slapping another man on the back, joking as they squeezed into the open air. Faye walked backward into the shadows, her heart racing.

The group of men seemed to breaking up, waving to one another as they walked off to their separate tents. She waited until the last one had his back to her and began to cross the dirt again.

She kept her broom by her side, sliding the chain behind, the best she could do to conceal it. When she got back to the mess tent entrance, she laid the chain to the side where no one would notice it, then she spun inside. It was empty. Someone would come by and turn off the generator soon, so she had to be quick. She unrolled the chain noisily across the plywood floor...

Chapter 52

Wyatt heard the sound of boots on dirt a second before he was lifted from the ground by the collar.

"What are you doing here?" A light turned on suddenly, directly in his eyes.

"Hey," Wyatt said, blinking in the harsh glare. He'd dropped his lethal box of toothpicks.

The man dropped Wyatt as quickly as he'd lifted him. The light shone briefly on the man's security badge, then back in Wyatt's face. "Who are you and what are you doing here?" The bounce of light off the truck gave Wyatt a sense of the man's bulk. His voice alone had the tenor of a linebacker.

Wyatt backed up against the fender. "God, you scared the shit out of me," he said, dusting off his pants.

"Answer my question."

"Sure, sure. I…I followed my friend out here, who, I'm sorry to say, snuck some gin into camp and got drunk. He's pretty loaded. I'm trying to find him."

The linebacker leaned into Wyatt's face. "You're the one I smell gin on."

"No, no, just one shot. Well, maybe two…"

The guard spun him around and pushed him against the fender. Wyatt felt his hands twisted and tied behind his back before he could resist.

Wyatt heard something hard strike the guard.

"Shit!" the guard yelled into the night. "What the hell? Who's out there? Are you really throwing stones at me, you drunken shithead?"

The guard pulled another zip-tie and anchored Wyatt's hands to the grill of the truck. "Hummph," he grunted.

Wyatt turned back toward his captor. The linebacker spun and shined his lamp where the stones had come from. He moved that way, toward a backhoe, stabbing his light into the darkness as he went.

Wyatt struggled against the plastic ties, to no avail. He yanked and rubbed them up and down the grill, but they were thick and tough. He watched as the guard crept carefully to the equipment. The guard shined his light to the right, turned it off, and ran to his left. Nice maneuver. But moments later Wyatt heard him curse and turn on his flashlight again. He mumbled as he circled fruitlessly behind the backhoe.

Suddenly, Wyatt felt his hands pulled down toward the ground. Relic squatted there, sawing the restraints with his hunting knife. "Let's go," he whispered. Wyatt smiled in the dark, shaking the sliced ties onto the ground.

As they stood and turned, the linebacker flicked on his light again, this time with a pistol in his right hand.

"Enough games," he growled. "Hands up."

Relic and Wyatt put their palms in the air.

The cough of a starting diesel reached their ears. The guard stepped back from them a bit and turned to look toward the mess tent.

Headlights on the bulldozer flashed to life as it ground into low gear and jolted forward. Within moments, the dozer was into another gear, whining up again for another shift when it lurched to a halt, its rear lifted and dumped back onto the ground. A terrible rending sound hung in the air for a second and then snapped. Lights on the mess tent wobbled and flickered in the night, then crashed to the earth like a string of disorganized dominoes, screaming, popping, exploding into darkness. Lights inside the tent became a misshapen mass as the canvas parachuted onto itself, a gigantic balloon imploding.

"I'll be gone to hell," Relic said, staring at the billowing, glowing tent.

The linebacker glared at Relic and Wyatt.

"Don't look at us," Relic said. "We're right here with you."

Wyatt turned his giggle into a snort.

"Stupid drunks."

Pop-pop! Sparks showered above the waving canvas. Relic touched Wyatt's shoulder and quietly led them one step backwards.

Someone yelled "Fire!"

The guard glanced behind him but Relic and

Wyatt were gone. He holstered his pistol and ran
toward the noise, yelling into his walkie-talkie for
help.

****

Arnulfo stepped outside of his tent and stared
at the spectacle, his mouth hanging open. The
thought of marshmallows popped into his mind,
and once he started laughing, he could not seem
to stop.

Chapter 53

The tent became a dome of light, then began to smolder and burst into flame near the back, near the kitchen stove.

"Hey, we just cleaned the grill back there," Relic said, making Wyatt laugh.

The fire spread slowly, casting a halo of light across the camp. Security guards hollered, workers yelled their curses and questions, and everyone rushed to see what the commotion was all about.

"Is she really crazy enough to do that?" Wyatt asked.

"Yep," Relic nodded.

"Well, shee-it," Wyatt did his best imitation of Faye.

Relic smiled. "Don't let her hear you or she'll knock your block off."

"No doubt."

"Would you see what you can do to slow down that backhoe up ahead of us and anything else with a lock and key? Then work your way north, swing back toward the staircase and we can meet up there."

Wyatt nodded.

"Keep a close look out. They'll be searching as soon as the mess is under control."

"What's your next move?" Wyatt asked.

Relic jerked his thumb toward the portable toilets.

"Really?" Wyatt said.

Relic turned and faded into the dark. Wyatt heard footfalls, someone moving quickly toward him. After a moment, he recognized her shape bobbing along. She tossed something and he heard it clacking into the bed of a pickup. She nearly ran into him.

"Hey." He put his hands out toward her.

"Hey," she said, slowing, but only a bit. "Here." She tossed a stick of dynamite to him, the fuse sparkling lit.

"Shit!"

"Throw it!" she shouted as she ran past. "Now!"

Wyatt stared at the tube in his hand. The fuse sputtered and spat and shortened with every second, time compressed with the tightness of his breath, the glowing fuse moving forward immutably until something like a spinning clutch popped in his chest and muscle movement became possible again. He reached his arm back and threw it as far and as fast as he could, then he spun and ran to the side of another truck and turned back to look.

The pickup Faye had tossed something into rose into the air with a smack that washed away all other sound, then fell back to the ground with a nasty twist as pieces of sheet metal dropped from the sky.

"Holy..."

Wyatt's stick of dynamite exploded somewhere beyond another truck, lighting something on fire, sending a second sonic boom through his skull, making him jump in his tracks. He stared at the blaze as it settled into a steady burn and looked the direction Faye had run.

A third, fourth, and fifth explosion erupted in quick succession in the row of portable toilets and Wyatt knew it was Relic's work. Where was Relic's peaceful resistance now? Lord, he hoped no one was in those toilets. Then, he thought, what a mess of shit, and he giggled and smacked his hands together.

Oh, my god, was it possible to have so much fun? He never expected stopping Lord Winnieship from stealing this canyon to feel so damn good.

He stared at the fire he'd started and tried to think. He wanted to follow Faye but there was no telling what other mayhem she had in mind, and he did not want to walk into an exploding outhouse. He tried to regulate his breathing, with only a little luck. He circled away from the path Faye had taken, giving her a wide berth, moving to the outer edge of the parked vehicles.

Wyatt turned and trotted toward a lone backhoe, maybe sixty yards away. Though the electric lights of the compound were out, the kitchen and dining room blaze cast a sallow glow on the tops of the other tents and equipment. The upper arm of the yellow backhoe was lit like a candle.

His shins scraped across brittle sage and he slowed to a walk. He'd lost his own toothpicks, so that trick would not work with the heavy equipment. After Faye's dynamite, toothpicks seemed pretty pathetic anyway. Maybe there was a set of keys kept in the ignition that he could toss away. Or maybe he could flatten its tires or pull wires from under the dash to disable the beast. He turned to watch the bobbing of flashlights all around the burning mess tent a quarter of a mile away. The voices of men rose and fell in a rhythm that was almost musical, like an offbeat composition.

He stopped at the base of the backhoe and stared up at the top, where the boom and dipper attached. He circled the machine to the open cabin and peered inside.

"Stop and turn around." The voice was deep and familiar.

Wyatt turned and raised his hands. Even in the semi-dark, Lynch's muscled bulk identified him immediately. He held a pistol aimed at Wyatt's chest.

"You!" Lynch said. "You sonofabitch."

Wyatt saw the left hook a milli-second before it struck his jaw, wrenching his head away and toward the ground. He stumbled to the side. A blow to his stomach struck like a rocket and his chest ached, all the veins in his body shut down by a sonic boom. Slivers of light flashed through his eyes, closed tight against the assault. He sensed himself floating to the earth, his muscles turned to liquid. He was out before he hit the dirt.

Chapter 54

Wyatt's jaw ached. He struggled to expand his breath, to ship vital oxygen to his brain and heart. Voices bounced around him but his mind could not assemble them into any meaning. Slowly, he began to recognize Lynch's hard-edged words, Schmidt's urgency, and Winford's confident tone.

"The tent fire's under control…" Schmidt said.

"We've got spot lights on the area and we're working through it," Lynch said.

"Hey, he's coming around," Schmidt said.

Wyatt blinked and opened his eyes a narrow crack. He managed a deeper gulp of air and began to feel his fingers and toes again. He realized he was sitting in one of those foldable canvas camping chairs. His wrists were tied to the arms, his ankles to the metal legs.

"Wyatt, I know you can hear me." It was Winford. "Take a minute to think about your situation here."

Wyatt opened his eyes wider. They were in

Winford's deluxe tent, larger than the rest of them, with room for an air mattress, folding table, camp chairs, and battery powered lamps. The same tent they'd all been together in days ago, when Wyatt had been excused and then heard their talk when they thought he was gone.

"You need to tell us just what you are up to," Winford said, pacing slowly over the ground, hands clasped behind his back.

"You know better than I," Wyatt said, the sound of his own voice weak and disappointing to him. He cleared his throat and sat up straighter.

"Let's review the facts." Winford spoke like it was closing argument in a courtroom. "First, you eavesdrop on our conversation." He motioned to Lynch and Schmidt, who sat behind him. "Then, when Lynch approaches you in the dining hall to discuss this with you, you run like a fugitive."

Wyatt tried to ignore the pain radiating from his jaw.

"Then, you take a series of desperate acts with a stranger unknown to all of us, or to anyone working on the project. Your accomplice. You jump into the river and even swim through class III rapids just to avoid a conversation with one of the project partners. You re-appear hiking along the cliffs to the north side of the canyon and flee again, like a man who knows he is guilty."

Wyatt started to respond, then stopped himself.

"When a security guard tries to question you, your unknown accomplice shoots him in the foot, wounding him for life. He's a kick boxing champion, Wyatt. His lost earnings, pain and suffering, and related damages exceed what you will earn in a decade."

Wyatt knew Winford was presenting their narrative, twisting the facts in subtle but important ways, trying it on for size, seeing how it would play to a judge or jury.

"With the help of your accomplice, you locate a cave and try to hide there. When Lynch finds you, you flee again. When he follows you to a passageway, you fire a gun at his face as he's calling out to you, forcing him to retreat. You nearly take his head off."

Winford was in fifth gear now, pacing and moving his hands to accentuate his points. "You get away, but that wasn't your real plan, was it? You return to the project here, under cover of night, and sabotage the mess tent, explode the vehicles, our supplies. You and your accomplice had to have planned this from the very start, a conscious, pre-meditated plan to injure or kill those who got in your way and to destroy a resort that will bring hundreds of jobs to this economy." Winford stopped and folded his arms across his chest. "This is what we know to be true, Wyatt. Now, we need you to answer a few important questions."

Wyatt's head pounded.

"Who is this accomplice of yours? What is your motive for these despicable acts? Revenge against me or the firm? Did you think you should have been paid more or been promoted, that we were holding you back unfairly? Have you become radicalized somehow, another 'homegrown' terrorist fighting against the American dream?"

Lynch and Schmidt both leaned forward intently.

"I know better than to talk to you," Wyatt said, his eyes leveled on Winford.

"Really, Wyatt? You know better," he huffed. "What a joke. Let me tell you what's going to happen to you, son,"

"I am not your son," Wyatt interrupted.

Winford ignored him. "First, you have lost your job and your career already. You can go with a mild reprimand from the firm and the bar association, or you can go out hard, facing disbarment. Second, you face criminal prosecution for so many offenses I can't even list them all. Malicious mischief and theft, destruction of private property, assault, battery, attempted murder, conspiracy to commit acts of terrorism."

Winford let his words float in the air.

Chapter 55

Bile rose in Wyatt's throat with a surge of anger and he felt his face redden. He took a breath through his mouth and let it out slowly through his nose. He thought about all that had happened since he'd come to this little canyon, not just the events, but how he saw Winford and how he saw himself. The acts of terrorism were not his, but Winford's, and they were close and personal and powerful. He had to move out of the dependent cycle he was in with Winford and the firm, his struggle for a piece of all that represented. Despite all his artful speeches, Winford had a hollow chest and a thirst for wealth. And Wyatt now understood, more deeply than he'd expected, how special this canyon was and how fragile it was under the iron hand of a man like Winford.

"I know you're testing out your little narrative there," Wyatt said, choosing his words carefully, "but it's full of blind assumptions and mischaracterizations that are way out of line."

"Then enlighten us," Winford said.

"I'm not saying anything else to any of you."

"You little shit." Lynch lunged forward and grabbed Wyatt by his shirt, lifting him and his chair from the ground.

"Stop it." Schmidt put his hand on Lynch's arm.

Lynch dumped Wyatt back on the ground. The chair teetered, then rested upright. Lynch landed a solid punch to Wyatt's stomach and stepped back. Wyatt gasped for air, his mind again on the edge of consciousness. He forced his lungs to expand despite the pain and took deeper and deeper breaths.

The three men stood and watched him.

Wyatt looked up at Lynch. "Like all cowards, you're a bully."

Lynch's right hook landed squarely on Wyatt's cheek and nose, crunching cartilage, breaking capillaries, and flooding his face and mouth with blood. "Tell me where your partner in crime is hiding or the next one will be worse," Lynch said.

"Not so hard," Schmidt said under his breath.

"Screw you," Lynch replied.

Wyatt tried to clear the haze from his vision. He spat blood onto the ground and looked up again at Lynch.

"I don't know where he is now,"

Lynch raised his right fist again.

"But I know where he's going next."

Schmidt put his hand on Lynch's arm and lowered it.

"That's better," Winford said.

Wyatt took a breath. "He's working his way to your precious petroglyphs."

Chapter 56

"How do they know about the petroglyphs?" Winford asked.

"Fuck if I know," Lynch said.

"Let's step out of the tent, gentlemen." Schmidt escorted them outside.

They walked several yards away, watching the front of the tent as they went.

"We have to find this accomplice," Winford said.

"No shit, Sherlock," Lynch scowled.

"Right, guys, and now we know exactly how to do it," Schmidt said. "We get to the petroglyphs right away. If we get there first, of course, we lay a trap. If he's there ahead of us, we block his escape."

Lynch nodded.

"I'll leave the logistics to you gentlemen," Winford said, turning to leave.

"You know shit about logistics and we're in charge of this, not you," Lynch spat.

"Right, right," Schmidt said to them both.

"You want to meet with your security team?" he asked Lynch, changing the subject.

Lynch glared at Winford and reached for the walkie-talkie on his belt. "Security team, this is alpha-one, alpha-one to security team. Everyone meet me outside the mess tent in ten or pick up your pink slip."

****

Wyatt closed his eyes and his world began to swirl. He hung his head between his knees and looked at the hard-packed dirt until the spinning stopped. He could hear urgent whispers from outside the tent, too distant to make out the words. He hoped he'd done the right thing, leading them to the petroglyphs. Relic was headed there, but smart enough to spot Lynch, wily enough to stay away from him. Probably, Lynch would leave him here in Winford's tent, tied up and maybe gagged. But he'd have some hope of escape from here. And that meant some hope of searching Winford's tent. He needed to find something to incriminate the man, to prove the fraud, and not just stop the project, but dismantle it.

He thought of Relic, probably trotting all over the canyon. He wondered what was happening with Faye. Those soft brown eyes hid a real fireball, hell and havoc in a kitchen smock. He found that smiling hurt his lips.

Movement behind him, at the rear of the tent, made him stiffen.

"Wyatt?"

Speak of the devil, he thought. He turned to hear her better. "Faye?"

"Yes, I'll get you out of here."

"Thank god you're OK." He took a breath. "No, wait." Wyatt knew what his idea really needed. "Faye?"

"Yes?"

"They're going to those petroglyphs up on the ridge, to the east."

"There are two ridges."

"Right, right, I forgot. The upper one, the one on the north, the one with the wooden staircase, where we agreed to meet Relic. You can't get up the ridge without them, at least not from that direction. Get to those stairs, but be careful. Lynch and those guys are going there too, up to the top. Warn him if you can."

"Sure. What more can I do?"

"We need to shut this down completely."

Faye was silent for a moment.

"We have to prove…"

The front tent flap opened suddenly and Schmidt walked in, his face somber. Lynch and Winford followed. Wyatt heard Faye slide the back of the canvas tent to the ground.

Chapter 57

Faye backed slowly on her hands and knees, away from the tent and the sound of Lynch's voice. To the stairs and the petroglyphs, to warn Relic, Wyatt had said. She knew she had to hurry.

She stood carefully, took a few more steps backwards, then turned and sprinted toward the three-sided shed, hoping a horse was there for the taking. She ran behind the row of workers' tents, trusting her feet to find the ground in the dark. Distant flashlights swung in dizzy, disjointed curves as men shouted across the camp: names, commands, obscenities, directions. To her left, she saw a lantern high on a wooden wall, lighting one side of the shelter. She angled toward it, but her foot snagged on something hard, propelling her down to the dirt, knocking the wind from her.

"Hmmph." She lay there for a moment to catch her breath. She rolled to her side, sat up, cross-legged, and got her bearings. Someone was moving directly toward her, lighting the ground by her feet. Too close now for her to run away.

"Who are you?" demanded a deep voice behind the flashlight.

She stood and dusted herself off. "Faye. I work the kitchen."

The man ran the light up and down, taking her measure. She raised her arm against the glare. "Who are you?"

He shined the lantern on his chest, illuminating Security" in bold letters on his shirt.

"Oh."

"What are you doing?" He moved the light to the ground between them.

"On my way to the mess tent, to see if I can help."

"It's that way," he pointed behind him.

"Right. I need a light, first." She pointed toward the lantern hanging on the horse shed.

"Get on with it, then. Go directly to the mess hall or you could be arrested." A remote voice hissed from the walkie-talkie on his belt. "Security two," the man answered, pushing a button, "behind the tents, then back toward the motor pool."

"All OK?" the voice asked.

He looked at Faye and hesitated for a moment. "All OK."

"Thanks," she waved curtly and trotted toward the shed, resisting the urge to look back, to make sure he was moving on.

Two horses were tied to a rope hung across the open side of the shed. They wore halters and lead ropes, but no bridles. She slowed her pace and began to mutter soothing words, keeping the

horses calm and quiet. She went to the lantern that
hung on the side and took it into the shelter, dimming it from security and anyone else who might
be watching from outside. She set the light near a
yellow case and turned to the horse closest to her,
a small gray, petting his nose and patting his neck.
She looked around one more time, untied the rope,
and slung it over the horse's neck. She hopped onto
the gray's back and wrapped her left hand into his
mane.

Her horse took a step sideways, adjusting to
her weight. She looked into the shed again and
at the lantern she'd set on the ground, its flame
pulsing against the amber case and this time she
recognized the four-starred design on the side. A
drone.

She knew she had to leave camp fast, but
something stopped her and she stared at the hard
case with the device that, she assumed, was inside.

"Well, shit." She slid back off of the gray, went
into the shed, and lifted the case, feeling the weight
of it. She went quickly back to the horse and
remounted.

A pair of flashlight beams crisscrossed the
ground near the back of the shed, rolling with the
sound of clomping boots, coming quickly toward
her. She used the lead rope as she would a half-set
of reigns and turned the gray away, kicking her
heels into his belly. The horse began a brisk walk
toward the row of shadowed tents.

The large tent at the end stood about a hundred yards away, lights shifting about outside, the
place where Wyatt was being held. She didn't like

leaving him, but if he was right, she knew where they were all going and she had to warn Relic. If she could find the stairs, she could let her horse loose there. She made a wide arc around the tent, her gray slowing over some rough ground, then moving faster along a well-worn trail leading east.

Chapter 58

Schmidt walked stiffly into the tent, his brow lined and taut as a rappeler's rope. Winford slid through the opening, sat in a camp chair, and released a puff of air. Lynch marched in, his eyes as hard as marbles. He pulled a switch blade from his pocket and opened it with a flick of his wrist. He moved directly to Wyatt.

Wyatt stiffened in his chair. Lynch knelt and cut loose Wyatt's legs, then stood and freed his hands. Wyatt looked at each of the men in turn, waiting for someone to say something.

"Stand up," Lynch said, closing the blade and tucking it away.

Wyatt looked at Winford, who kept his eyes on the ground. Wyatt stood and, before he could react, Lynch punched him in the stomach. He fell back into the chair and bent forward, wheezing for breath.

"That's a gentle reminder. No games, you ass-hole, or you'll find out what a real beating is. Now, stand up again and put your hands out in front of you."

Wyatt squeezed against his stomach muscles and slowly rose from the chair. Lynch grabbed Wyatt's hands and wrapped a zip-tie around them, binding them together.

"We'll go up first," Lynch said to the others. "You two follow. Bring a four-wheeler with you and tarps or blankets." Lynch and Schmidt exchanged a serious glance. "To wrap things in..."

Schmidt nodded. "Bring some guards to help?"

"No. Buttons is the only one I'd trust for that and he's out of action. I've told the rest of them to supervise the cleanup. Gotta keep these workers honest or our gear will start disappearing."

"Hmmph."

Lynch grabbed Wyatt's hands and pulled him out of the tent and into the night.

Wyatt stumbled over a rock and caught his balance. Lynch shined his flashlight ahead of them.

"Follow the light," Lynch said. "I'll be two steps behind you with my pistol ready." He shined the light in Wyatt's face, making him squint and blink. "Start moving."

Wyatt forced himself to put one foot before the other and began walking in the weak light. After a few yards, a trail appeared and Wyatt followed it forward. Lynch's feet seemed to pound the ground behind him, a monster keeping pace with Wyatt's every step.

The path wound gently toward the east, and Wyatt noticed a flush of rouge on the canyon rim.

The warmth of a new day was pushing hard against
the night, chasing it across the sky. The realization
that he'd been up all night made his bones feel like
lead. His ribs and head ached, and he longed for a
long cool drink of water and some rest.

The trail turned north, toward the massive
cliffs now becoming visible again in the distance.
He and Lynch wound steadily along, travelling
maybe a half-mile across the open flats. Blackness
seemed to rise from the grass like a fog. The dim
glow of sunrise began to grant shape and distance
to the landscape. Wyatt came to a familiar ridge
that rose about three hundred feet. The path ran
closely along the rock face and disappeared around
a corner to the right. Wyatt stopped and looked
back at Lynch.

"Keep going."

Wyatt resumed his pace and followed the
path as it turned and aimed directly at what looked
to be an impassible block of stone. There, at the
base, stood the series of wooden stairs and land-
ings, man-made switchbacks to the top of the cliff
that he and Relic had come down after viewing the
panel of petroglyphs. Wyatt stopped at the bottom
and leaned forward, catching his breath.

"Up." Lynch's voice was cold.

"A real chatter-box, you are," Wyatt said,
glancing behind him. Lynch's stare took every
speck of humor from the world and incinerated
it. Wyatt turned back and swallowed hard. He
trudged upward, every step feeling like a walk to
the gallows. He moved close to the railing and
pulled up with his arms for a few steps, then let

his hands drop back to his stomach. Tied together, it was easier not to use his hands on the railing at all. They reached the first platform and turned for the next series of stairs. It really could work as a hangman's scaffold, he thought.

Wyatt's knees felt like rubber by the time they reached the second platform. He rested against the rail and tried to regain some strength. Lynch stood right behind him, saying nothing. Lynch seemed not to be in any sort of rush, a realization that spread a bitter taste in Wyatt's mouth. Telling them that Relic was coming up here now seemed like the worst idea he'd ever had. And maybe the last idea he'd ever have.

Wyatt steeled himself for the final push to the top and began the climb. He concentrated on placing one foot before the other, sure to get fully onto each step before trying the next. When he reached the third platform, he leaned over the railing, draped himself over it, and panted for air.

Lynch was also breathing hard, but he moved past Wyatt and up the last two steps to the trail on top of the cliff. Wyatt watched from under his brow as Lynch disappeared for several moments. Wyatt wanted to flee down the stairs but even going down, he knew Lynch would catch him. At that moment, he heard the baritone hum of a vehicle. Schmidt drove a four-wheeler around the edge of the ridge below and turned toward the bottom of the stairs. Winford sat behind him on the squat machine. Any thought of escape Wyatt tried to harbor evaporated in the desert air.

Lynch re-appeared at the trailhead and

motioned with his pistol for Wyatt to get moving again. Wyatt shifted his weight back onto his legs and moved unevenly onto the trail. Lynch stood to the side and motioned Wyatt ahead.

Sunshine brightened on top of the ridge, sketching hard-angle shadows through the bushes. Wyatt wound his way along the path for maybe three hundred yards and came to the hard-packed clearing he and Relic had been on the day before. He moved to a rock along the side and fell to a seated position next to it.

Lynch looked around briefly. "Stay put. If you're not right here," he pointed to the ground, "I will find you, gut you, and string your intestines around your throat."

Wyatt could only stare as Lynch turned back along the trail and disappeared.

Chapter 59

The second pebble finally caught his attention, rolling toward him across the dust. Wyatt sat up straight and scanned the rock face in front of him. He looked to his right, then back to the trail on his left. No one. But the rock had come from somewhere. He watched the horizon in front of him for movement and then saw it: Faye, standing two hundred feet above, on the cliff above the clearing. He wanted badly to cry out, to warn her, to speak with her, but he stifled the urge. What was she doing up there?

She moved her palms in a downward motion, like an instruction to be still, or maybe to be quiet, and she disappeared.

Just seeing Faye made him feel whole again, like hope could exist in the universe. He listened intently as faint sounds of scratching and shuffling reached his ears. He heard people pushing through the bushes, tromping along the trail, and breaking out into the open. Schmidt and Winford must have joined Lynch at the top of the stairs so they could make their way here together.

Schmidt appeared first, glancing at Wyatt, then moving along the edge of the clearing toward the sandstone cliff. He leaned against the rock and folded his arms.

Winford stepped into the open ground and eyed Wyatt with deep suspicion. He glanced at Schmidt, walked toward Wyatt, and sat on a low rock a few feet away from him.

Lynch stood near the trailhead, scanning the area.

Without warning, Winford reached forward and slapped Wyatt in the face.

Wyatt felt a burn across his cheeks and squeezed his eyes shut for a moment. Then he raised his head and clenched his mouth into a firm line. He looked straight at Winford, daring him to do it again. Winford stood this time and put his weight into a second slap, spinning Wyatt's head away.

"Name your accomplice or I'll keep doing this all day," Winford said.

Wyatt rubbed the pain from his jaw and watched Winford from the corner of his eye. Winford was a wimp at this, compared to Lynch.

"I'll tell you the whole story, but…" Wyatt guessed at how it had happened. "It starts with you."

Winford sat back onto the rock and glared at him.

"It started when you swindled an old man out of his ranch."

Winford's eyes widened.

"Or, at least this part of his ranch," Wyatt motioned with his bound hands. "You knew how valuable this real estate could be. When the old man died, you had the most important piece of your plan."

"You lying shit…" Winford raised his palm to strike Wyatt again.

"No, I've seen it, Winford. I've seen the whole file, remember? Cal Snow and the Western Investments Company create Little Horse Canyon, LLC. But you own Western, don't you? You were in a contract with Snow – with your own client. You pony up $150,000 to capitalize it, but you probably never paid that much, did you?"

Winford put his hand back down.

"No, you probably gave Snow a fraction of that. But the interesting thing about the management agreement? On the death of Snow, Western Investments got all of the shares and all the property held by the LLC. And you advised Snow to deed his land to the LLC, in exchange for your paltry investment. The land is worth millions. And after all the documents were signed, all you had to do was wait. How old was Snow when he signed? 90? 95? Was he even capable of understanding all those documents?"

Winford's glare would have etched glass.

"That's fraud in the inducement, Winford, you know that. The whole deal goes down the tubes. Fraud, misrepresentation, violation of a dozen rules of ethics, enough to get even the great Todd Winford the Fourth disbarred."

Winford leapt from his seat and struck Wyatt again, splitting his lip. The iron taste of blood filled his mouth and he spat it out. "I knew it," Wyatt said, wiping his lips.

"I've done what I need to succeed, you little shit," Winford said. "That old man was broke. I gave him the cash he needed, right when he needed it, and he got to keep his ranch until he died. No one else did that, and no one else has the vision to make this canyon into what it's really worth. When I'm done with this, the place will be famous, and Raptor Canyon will put its partners into an early and wealthy retirement." Winford glanced at Schmidt, who nodded.

Wyatt looked for Lynch, but he was out of sight.

"This is a beautiful and complex canyon," Wyatt said. "But it's remote. How are you going to get people all the way out here? For a luxury hotel and a spa? They can get that anywhere. If you think you can get wealthy off this little canyon, you're out of your mind."

"You're a fucking idiot, Wyatt. I don't know how you ever got hired on at the firm in the first place."

"Top ten in my class…" Wyatt said.

"You think you're so smart," Winford said. "Who's sitting in the dirt with his hands tied up, bleeding like a pig? Honestly, Wyatt, you look like death warmed over. Your hair's matted to your head like glue, your pants are all torn up, your shirt's soaked with sweat, your face is black and blue. So much for your brilliant career, son. I really don't think you were cut out to work for me, from the beginning."

"That much turns out to be very true," Wyatt said with a hint of pride, staring at Winford. For just a second, Wyatt felt sorry for the man.

"You know damn well what will make this canyon famous." Winford nodded and looked at Schmidt, who didn't move. "But maybe you need another look. Stand up."

Wyatt stared at him.

"Come on, now, stand up."

Wyatt put his hands on the rock next to him and lifted himself off the ground. He stood fully upright, determined not to let Winford see him wince.

"Over there," Winford pointed away from the trailhead.

Wyatt stretched his neck and moved toward the far side of the rock wall. As he shuffled closer, he saw the two petroglyphs of warriors he'd seen earlier, with what looked like shields in front of them. Above them were a collection of images resembling lizards or even alligators. Among them was the skull of a raptor he and Relic had examined. The skull was larger than a falcon's and instead of the beak of a bird, the teeth of a dinosaur shone in the morning sun. He reached his fingers toward it.

"Don't touch it," Winford said.

"So this is what fake petroglyphs look like?" Wyatt asked.

Winford's cheeks reddened. "In fact, these are the first and only verified petroglyphs of dinosaurs. This is going to turn archeology on its head. Visitors and tourists from around the country, even from around the world, will want to see this in their lifetimes."

Wyatt stared at the petroglyphs and thought again about Winford's plan. "Fucking diabolical," he nearly whispered. "I'll give you that."

"Thank you."

Chapter 60

A shriek from above shocked Wyatt, and he moved quickly back from the petroglyphs and looked up.

Schmidt ran to Wyatt and pulled him by his bindings back to the rock where he'd been sitting. "Down." Schmidt pushed on Wyatt's shoulder and he fell hard into the dust. Schmidt and Winford moved closer to the trailhead and waited.

A gush of curses erupted from somewhere in the bushes as the commotion moved closer to the clearing.

"…stomp on your balls, tear out your eyes, you little pervert," Faye yelled.

Wyatt's throat tightened and he stood back up. Faye twisted back and forth, yanking, resisting, grunting with effort as Lynch shoved her onto the open ground. Hands tied behind her back, she could not break her fall and landed hard on her side.

"Shit," Wyatt said.

"Who the hell is this?" Winford demanded.

"Found her up there," Lynch waved above the petroglyphs, "watching us."

"I recognize her. She works in the mess tent," Schmidt said. "She's kitchen help."

"This is your accomplice?" Winford asked.

Faye groaned quietly and curled into a ball. Long, dark hair hid her face.

"No, I don't know her." Wyatt sat back onto the ground.

"Don't bullshit a bullshitter," Winford said.

"She's in this somehow," Lynch said, "but there's somebody else. The one I chased into the river, along with Wyatt, was a man. About average height, black hair, ponytail, quick little bastard. Definitely not her though." He pointed to Faye.

Lynch, Schmidt and Winford walked toward each other and spoke rapidly in low tones, asking themselves who could have turned the camp upside down, collapsed the mess tent, set it on fire, jerry-rigged the trucks and locks.

While they spoke, Faye swung the hair from her face and twisted around. Her brow crinkled with a touch of fear until she saw him, then her coffee-colored eyes glowed and her lips parted into a smile, and Wyatt suddenly knew exactly what she looked like as a little girl.

"...he's your problem, Winford, so you get something out of him," Lynch was saying, "or I'll get something out of you."

Schmidt stepped between them, and Lynch turned aside.

"I'm going to circle around and check for

signs of anyone else," Lynch said. "Christ, we got a whole damned gang of them out there." He clamped his hands into fists and stomped away from the clearing. Schmidt and Winford looked at each other for a moment.

Winford strode to where Wyatt sat in the dirt and began to scream. "You sorry sonofabitch!" Winford kicked Wyatt again and again, striking his legs, stomach and butt. Powerless again before Winford's wrath, Wyatt held his arms to his head, squinting, squirming with pain, working hard not to cry out. Winford swung his legs in pure, wild anger, wailing all the while until he finally stepped away, exhausted. When Wyatt realized the blows had stopped, he opened his eyes and watched Winford circle away, kicking the dust now, cursing Wyatt's bloodline to the beginning of time.

Winford's tirade wound down and he stood watching across the distance, catching his breath. He turned toward Wyatt and walked back toward him in cold silence. Winford's face seemed stretched like leather on a drum, his lips in a grimace, his usual aloofness gone.

"You are going to tell us about the man who is working with you or I am going to let Lynch beat you to death. With rocks." Winford stopped a few feet from Wyatt and stared down at him.

Wyatt looked for Lynch, but could not find him. Faye sat up slowly and crossed her legs, her hands still tied behind her back. Schmidt stood with his arms crossed, watching Winford, a touch of amusement on his lips. Wyatt figured that Schmidt had never seen Winford lose his cool.

Neither had Wyatt. Maybe, he thought, he had an opening here.

Wyatt took a breath and looked at Winford. "You mean, the guy who saw you and your partners murder a man?"

Winford's pale eyes narrowed.

"Right here." Wyatt pointed to the clearing. "Murdered just a few days ago. Right, Schmidt?"

Schmidt's expression turned cold, his lips tight against his teeth.

"How does he know?" Winford spun toward Schmidt.

"He doesn't, you idiot, he's baiting us."

"That's not bait." Winford pointed at Wyatt. "He's not guessing. He knows what happened. How? Wyatt was with me, the whole time you—"

"No..."

"Shut up," Winford moved quickly to Schmidt's face and shook his finger. "This is all your doing."

Wyatt pivoted on his rear and scrabbled a few feet closer to Faye.

Schmidt took a step back and raised his palms in the air. "Don't be an idiot—"

"I'm tired of your bullshit," Winford said, advancing another step.

Lynch strode out of the brush that ran along the trail and moved between Wyatt and Faye.

Relic followed Lynch by several yards, keeping hidden from him, leaving the saplings between them.

"Wyatt knows, damn it," Winford said to Schmidt. "How could that happen unless you and your goon screwed it all up?"

Chapter 61

Lynch's skin flushed and his face boiled into a wrathful sneer, his profile more like an ape than man. He moved into Schmidt's field of view, un-holstered his Walther P4 and held it by his side.

Surprised, Schmidt turned away from Winford and lifted his palms toward Lynch.

"Well," Winford said, his customary arrogance returned. "Have you found the missing asshole?"

"He was never missing," Lynch said, raising his gun toward Winford.

Wyatt and Faye looked at each other. Wyatt mouthed the words, "Go low."

Schmidt angled part way in front of Winford, shielding him, waving his hands. "Wait!"

The P4 jerked with the explosion and a spray of blood burst from Schmidt's right arm. Winford seemed to fly backward of his own volition.

Wyatt stood part way up, his knees flexed. Faye rolled quickly toward Lynch's left foot, slamming tightly against it. As Lynch began to look down at her, to his left, Wyatt lowered his shoulder and rammed into Lynch's right side with all the force he could muster.

Lynch's fingers loosened on the pistol and he toppled sideways to the ground, his legs pinned by Faye, his shoulder crunched hard against the ground by Wyatt. The pistol slid across the dust. Wyatt crashed ungracefully on top of them both.

Faye rolled from under them and stood up. Wyatt got his legs under himself, but in the effort to stand, accidently flung himself backward into the dust.

Lynch's eyes were closed and his hands searched blindly over the dirt. Wyatt tried again and stood upright this time. He rushed for Lynch's left arm and began to twist it. Lynch rolled onto his stomach and Wyatt used the strength of the ties on his hands to leverage Lynch's arm toward his back. But Lynch moved his right hand under his chest and lifted himself with a one-arm push-up.

Relic slid his pack to the ground.

Wyatt lost what leverage he had as Lynch tore free.

Relic leapt from the brush, feet drumming, arms churning, sprinting straight at them so close and hot Wyatt flinched, then Relic twisted head-long into Lynch, his knee aimed at the last second like a battering ram, all of his weight behind it, pounding Lynch's temple into the ground. Lynch went suddenly limp.

Wyatt pushed himself off Lynch's back and knelt next to him. Sweat fell like raindrops from his cheeks and into the dust. He stared at Lynch's back for a moment, then at Relic, and nodded. Wyatt turned to look for the others.

"Lay still," Faye said. She had moved to Schmidt, who sat wounded in the center of the clearing. He stared into the distance, a man in shock.

Wyatt reached for the P4 and stood up. He shuffled toward Schmidt and raised the pistol uneasily. Relic walked to Wyatt and put his hand gently onto the gun and clicked something on it.

"Let's leave the safety on, for now," he said.

Wyatt lowered the gun and nodded.

Relic drew his hunting knife and cut the ties on Wyatt's hands. He moved to Faye and cut hers too, then turned the handle toward her. She took the knife and cut Schmidt's shirt sleeve off.

Schmidt's skin lost its color as the initial shock seemed to settle in. Worry sculpted his eyes and lips as he watched Faye tie the sleeve into a tourniquet just below his shoulder.

Relic took his knife back from Faye and walked over to Lynch, who was still unconscious. Relic went to his daypack and found a roll of nylon twine. He cut a piece and tied Lynch's hands tightly behind his back.

Wyatt went to Winford, who lay flat on his back. Wyatt held his hand to Winford's nose and felt the flow of breath. A cup-sized circle of blood soaked his left shoulder. Maybe the bullet had gone through Schmidt and hit Winford too.

"Wake up." Wyatt shook Winford firmly on his uninjured shoulder. Relic walked toward them, twine and hunting knife in hand.

"Try to sit him up," Relic said.

Wyatt moved behind Winford and lifted. The motion stirred Winford awake and he gasped for air. Wyatt pushed harder, until Winford was in a seated position. Relic tied one hand and pulled the other toward it, so he could tie them together.

Winford let a quick, high-pitched wail and slumped forward with a whimper. Relic moved Winford's hands closer and tied them firmly. Winford was half-awake now, aware only of his pain.

"Now what?" Wyatt asked.

Chapter 62

"They need a doctor," Faye said. "Bullet wounds and probably a concussion, if you haven't killed that one." She pointed at Lynch, who was still immobile.

"Let's see if we can get them down off this ridge," Relic said. He moved back to Lynch and tried to shake him awake. He rolled Lynch from his stomach to his side then onto his back and poured water over his face. Lynch began to mutter words, as if talking in his sleep, and pulled his feet to his chest.

"Some progress over here," Relic reported.

Wyatt squatted in front of Winford. "Hey, Lord Winnieford. Anyone in there? You've been shot, you ass, by your own partner. We've got to get you to medical help. Can you hear me?"

Faye watched them.

Winford's eyes began to open and focus on the ground before him.

"Can you hear me?"

"Yes, you fucking idiot, I wish I could not hear you." Winford was back.

"Yeah, well, you ought to taste your words before you spit them out. You're in a world of hurt and a world of trouble," Wyatt said.

Winford winced when he tried to bring his hand to his face.

"Don't move too much, you've been shot in the shoulder."

"My hands are tied. You've tied me up," Winford's voice rose a pitch.

"Come on, see if you can stand up."

"You are going to burn for this, son, and I mean burn."

Wyatt stepped back and watched him for a moment. "Winford, we know the whole story. You can't wiggle out of this one."

"Watch me."

"Wyatt?" Faye leaned toward him.

He turned to her.

"I found the drone and…it worked."

Wyatt stared at her, missing her meaning.

"The drone. It's up there, with a wide angle shot of the whole site and a voice recording." She pointed to the top of the cliff where she'd stood earlier. "It should still be recording now."

"But Lynch caught you…"

"I heard him coming. I went to him first, so he wouldn't find the drone."

"God, I love you," Wyatt beamed.

"I should hope so," she put her hand on her hip, her nose in the air in mock pride.

Wyatt turned to Winford. "Hear that, son?"

he mocked. "The whole thing on tape and video."
He tucked Lynch's pistol into his belt.

Winford's face went slack.

"Done talking at us for a while, are you?" Wyatt said, scooting behind him. He lifted Winford to his feet and helped him balance.

Relic touched Faye's shoulder. "Sorry I wasn't fast enough to help when muscle man grabbed you."

She shut her eyes for a moment and shook her head dismissively. "Your timing was right on."

"You sure put up a hell of a racket." Relic flashed a smile.

"Grandpa said I had a flair for it." Her lips curled in a playful smile and she spun and went to Schmidt. She put her arms under his uninjured shoulder and pulled him up.

"Why don't we get these two down off the ridge? While we can," Wyatt said to Relic.

Lynch was seated with his legs in front of him, moaning softly.

Relic put his pack back on. "Right. I'll be close behind you," he said.

Lynch blinked and looked around him. His icy eyes widened for a flash, then narrowed into tight slits when he saw Relic.

"Yeah," Relic nodded at Lynch. "Wyatt and me just walked right out of those caves, free as sparrows."

"Walk right on down the trail," Wyatt said to Winford, gently pushing him from behind. He and Faye walked Winford and Schmidt past the brush and down the path toward the wooden stairs.

"Wait, Wyatt. The drone," Faye whispered.

"Right. Go get it. I'll stay with them."

She hurried off the trail and onto a ledge of rock that led to a patch of bald sandstone. From there, she scrambled higher and out of sight.

They waited quietly for several minutes. When she returned, Faye held the drone case by her side and picked her way carefully back down the slick rock.

Back on the trail, she lifted the case like a trophy. She and Wyatt smiled at each other. He turned back to Winford and Schmidt and prodded them forward. The four made their way carefully down the steps.

They stopped to rest on the rocky trail at the bottom. Wyatt heard footfalls above them and looked up. Relic was guiding Lynch down the stairs. The four of them waited until Relic and Lynch reached the bottom.

They all spread out along the trail. The four-wheeler Winford and Schmidt had ridden in sat off to the side, key still in the ignition. Winford seemed to be walking fairly well. Schmidt was in serious pain, but shuffling at a steady pace. Lynch seemed to have no problem moving, but the fight was clearly out of him. His gaze focused some unknown yards ahead, hardly recognizing anything or anyone close to him.

"Winford, keep going," Relic said.

"What about that?" Winford complained, pointing at the four-wheeler.

"No, I think you guys have earned the right to walk back to camp," said Relic. "You know the way.

Stay on this trail as it rounds the corner up ahead, then you can see the tents from there. Schmidt, keep moving and you'll get there. Lynch, you too. People in the camp can get you to the nurse's station and some help."

Wyatt spread his hands, asking an unspoken question to Relic. Why let them walk back to camp by themselves?

Relic and Faye exchanged a quick glance. "Let's talk, once they're on their way," Relic said.

Wyatt looked at Winford and pointed down the trail. Winford's shoulders drooped. He nodded sullenly and turned away. As he went, Schmidt and Lynch fell in line behind him. Wyatt watched as they reached the turn in the trail and slowly disappeared around the edge of the high ridge.

Chapter 63

"Sit for a minute," Relic pointed to the bottom steps. Wyatt plopped onto the wooden stair and sucked a deep breath of morning air. Faye steadied herself on the railing and sat next to him.

"Oh, my god," Wyatt put his face in his hands.

"Well said," Faye agreed.

Relic removed his pack and pulled out a bag of candied peanuts. He displayed it as an offer, then poured the M&M's into their hands.

Wyatt chewed quickly, swallowed, and opened his hand for more. "Why didn't we take those guys back to camp? Find a way to contact the police?" Wyatt asked.

"At camp, they've got the rest of their team. They could jump us in a flash, we'd be outnumbered, outgunned." Relic put the candies away.

"Yes…"

"I'm not sure he's the sheriff's favorite, either," Faye added, looking at Relic.

Wyatt's brow rose.

"That's another story…" Faye's eyes rolled upward.

"It's not just me, though. I think we've all got to get out of here," Relic said. "Before Winnieship gets his arrogance back and the security guys show up here."

"I guess that's right," Faye sighed.

Wyatt looked up. "Where to?"

"Back to the ranch." Faye tucked her hair behind her ears. "We can call for help from there. Rest up. Get some food. Make sure the drone recorded what we need, and get it to the sheriff."

Relic stroked his goatee. "Good. You can take a couple of horses from the corral."

"You're going somewhere else?" Faye asked.

"I have a couple more things to take care of first, and, yes, I think I'll head north for a while." Relic glanced toward the high cliffs.

"Come meet us at the ranch later?"

"If I can."

Wyatt expelled a puff of air. Relic and Faye looked at him.

"My career at the firm is long over, but…"

"What?" Faye asked.

"I'd like my first independent case to be the one that gets this canyon back to you, back as part of your grandfather's ranch."

Faye's eyes watered for a moment, then she blinked them dry. "Thank you."

"Only seems right."

"I knew I liked you the moment I saw you," Relic said to Wyatt.

"You hated me the moment you saw me."

"I got over it," Relic smiled.

"Let's go get those horses." Faye stood and embraced Relic. "Take care of yourself and come see me, 'uncle.'"

Wyatt stood and offered his hand. Relic hugged him instead and they patted each other on the back. Faye veered away from the trail and toward the corrals that sat about a mile to the northwest. She swung the drone gently in her left hand with each step. Wyatt nodded to Relic as he turned to follow her.

"Now," Relic said to himself, rubbing his hands together. He went to the four-wheeler and searched the supply trunk. "This ought to do."

Relic unwound the chain he'd found and took one end to the base of the stairs and tied it to the main support post. He walked the chain back to the four-wheeler and attached it to the back frame with a carabiner. He shouldered his pack and stared at the machine.

"Damned contraption is gonna do us some good today."

He sat in the padded seat and started the engine. Moving back and forth, he maneuvered the four-wheeler to face away from the stairs and inched forward until the chain was nearly tight. He gunned the engine, popped the clutch, and sprung ahead until the chain jerked the vehicle backward. The engine stalled, so he tried several times more until, finally, the four-wheeler kept moving forward, past the point where the post had held before, tearing the wood from its base, tugging the support sideways and out from under the stairs.

Pine beams tore and squealed, nails ripped and
popped apart in an explosion of noise. He turned
to look behind him. The main post had caught the
outer beam as it pulled apart. The clean, straight
lines of the staircase twisted into a Salvador Dali
painting, the design impossible, the steps writhing
out and downward as if gravity had inverted. The
structure buckled near the top and spilled onto
itself in a chaos of white pine and pixie sticks. He
closed his mouth and eyes as dust billowed around
him.

Chapter 64

Lynch trudged along the trail, head lowered, the sun baking the back of his neck. Schmidt and Winford followed him around the edge of the ridge, their feet sliding across the ground like prisoners on their way to execution. Lynch stopped and stared at the distant camp. The mess tent was still down and smoldering, workers trotting from place to place, the motor pool a jumble of shapes. Now and then, a random shout reached his ears. Schmidt and Winford stopped behind him.

Lynch struggled against the twine around his wrists, increasing his efforts, swaying and pulling and spinning in vain. His face flushed cherry red and he cursed without discipline, a forty-foot wave of venom crashing through his clenched teeth, more than mere words, more than mere expletives, they were animal grunts electrified by vile and hatred and frustration.

Schmidt and Winford took a step away, turning their faces to the ground.

Lynch's voice became hoarse with exhaustion. He knelt on one knee and panted like a bulldog.

Schmidt looked up at Winford and out at the camp. The bullet had gone through soft tissue near his shoulder and though he'd lost some blood, the tourniquet stemmed the flow. Still, his face was a pale gray, his lanky form stiff and unsteady. He cradled the arm at his elbow and grimaced.

Winford straightened his back and took a deep breath. His shoulder hurt like the devil but the wound was not deep. Though mostly by accident, Schmidt had literally taken a bullet for him. Winford struggled against the twine that tied his hands and yelped in pain. God, he needed a drink.

Lynch's tirade had vented everyone's despair and loosened their dire mood, moving it a notch away from utter defeat. They all felt a sliver of rising anger.

"Let's get moving again," Schmidt said.

Lynch rose slowly and turned toward them. "Back to camp and free of these ropes." His face was still pink with exertion. "No more time to waste." He spun back to the trail and began an awkward trot to the camp, his arms swaying together behind him. Winford and Schmidt hurried along.

Nearly thirty minutes later, Lynch reached the spot where Winford's deluxe tent stood, at the eastern edge of the tent city. He could see someone carrying tools, moving toward him.

"Hey, you!" Lynch shouted.

The man pointed to himself, the question implicit in his movement.

"Yes, you, come here."

He set his tools on the ground and walked quickly toward Lynch. Schmidt and Winford shuffled behind Lynch as they all moved to Winford's tent.

"What's your name?" Lynch asked.

"Tony." The young man wore faded jeans and a western style shirt, faux pearl snaps on the cuffs and pockets. A Broncos football team hat shaded his face.

"Tony, get a knife and cut us loose." Lynch turned to show him his bound hands.

Tony's eyes widened and he stopped short.

"No time to explain. You know who I am?" Lynch asked.

"Yes, sir. Chief of security."

"Right. So get us loose of these right now!"

Tony seemed to shake himself awake. He twisted his cap so it was backward on his head and moved close to Lynch. He pulled a pocket knife from his pants and began sawing at the tough nylon.

"Him too," Lynch said.

Winford offered his binding to Tony, who cut him loose. Tony moved to Schmidt and saw that his hands were not bound. Blood soaked his left shoulder and arm, which Schmidt held with care. Tony swallowed his question.

Lynch rubbed his wrists and looked about the camp. "Tony, what do you do here?"

"Labor. I'm working with the carpenters, mostly."

"Want a raise?"

Tony's blue eyes flashed.

"Double what you make now."

"Yes, sir."

"You work for security now. Get as many men as you can to gather the pickup trucks here, in fifteen minutes."

Tony shifted his feet and took a breath. "Sir, most of the equipment won't start. The ignitions are all monkey wrenched."

"What?"

"Sounds like somebody stuck stuff into the keyholes. We can't get but two of them started, as far as I can tell."

"Son." Winford stepped forward. "Get us something to drink, would you?"

Tony turned toward the center of camp, ready to fetch them drinks.

Lynch stiffened his back. "Wait," he said to Tony. "You should have water in your tent…" he told Winford.

Tony stopped and looked at Lynch.

"Something cold, lemonade and gin, maybe."

Schmidt nudged Winford, who ignored him.

"We've been tied up and tortured by the same people who attacked our camp. We're dehydrated," Winford complained.

"The generators are down," Tony said to them.

"So?" Winford said.

"Is Stella still on the security radio?" Lynch asked.

"Don't know about that…" Tony said.

"Lemonade?"

"Fuck your lemonade, Winford," Lynch said.

"No generators, no coolers, no lemonade," Tony said flatly. He looked to Lynch for reassurance.

"Thank god, Winford, that settles the lemonade issue. Can we get focused here?" Lynch said.

"Sure. Let's focus on the asshole who shot us." Winford glared at Lynch.

"The radio…" Schmidt said.

"Right, I already asked about that," Lynch said.

"Could you radio for some more help? Some backup?" Schmidt asked.

"Get us some chairs," Winford said to Tony.

Tony glanced around, uncertain where to find them.

"I know some guys, sure, but…" Lynch said.

"That will take too long," Winford said.

"Shut up," Lynch and Schmidt spoke in unison.

"We've already radioed for help," Tony said.

The three men stared at the young man standing in front of them.

"What?"

"Somebody already radioed the sheriff. They should have people here in another hour or so."

"Shit." Lynch turned away from Tony.

"I told you it would take too long for your guys…" Winford said.

"We don't want the sheriff?" Tony asked.

"We've got to get moving," Schmidt said.

"We can't wait for the sheriff or they'll get clean away," Lynch spoke to Tony, then looked at

Schmidt and Winford. "We have to take care of this ourselves." Lynch smacked a fist into his palm.

"Who's left from security?" Schmidt asked.

"Button's hurt," Lynch shook his head at the ground. "Cutter and Kowalski are at the caverns." He looked at Tony. "Find the other security officers, if you can. Greene, Schiller, and O'Leary."

"Wait. Weapons too," Schmidt announced.

"Shit, yes, Tony, we need rifles and pistols," Lynch said. "These assholes we're chasing are armed."

Tony's eyes swelled like jumbo marbles, blue orbs darting from Schmidt to Lynch and back again.

"I need medical attention," Winford said, to no one in particular.

"But we're not chasing anyone if we don't get some god damned wheels," Lynch yelled and pointed toward the motor pool. "Get us whatever trucks are running, Tony. Get whoever will help and get them here."

Tony took a slow step backward and glanced toward the center of camp. He looked like a schoolboy hoping desperately to be excused from class.

"Pronto."

Tony whirled and ran toward the collapsed mess tent and the row of trucks beyond.

. . . .

Chapter 65

Wyatt and Faye heard a squeal like fingernails on glass and a distant thump. They turned behind them to see the wooden staircase ripped from the face of the cliff, a jumble of toothpicks in a haze of dust.

Faye grinned.

Wyatt nodded at Relic in the distance.

They turned back toward the corrals and hurried.

A shed of rough-cut wooden slats anchored the northern end of the rails. The fence curved in semi-circles from either side of the shed and came together at a gate on the opposite side. As they came closer, they saw an old Ford 150 pickup parked on shallow ground by the gate and a man leaning against the hood, his hat low on his head, one boot propped on a crooked fender.

Wyatt slowed to a walk. "Faye?"

She waved him back. "It's OK. I know him."

The man slid his hat higher on his head and

watched as she moved toward him.

"Hola," she said.

"Hola, Faye," he said, pushing away from the truck.

"Arnulfo, good to see you." Faye reached out her hand.

He shook it quickly. "Good to see you too."

"What's going on?" she asked.

"That is my question to you." He waved his arm toward Wyatt and the far cliff behind him.

She put her hand on her hip and cast him a sideways glance.

He grinned. "I liked the fireworks, my friend. Even roasted a couple of marshmallows."

She blew a sigh from her lungs. "These are bad people, Arnulfo." She pointed south toward the tent city. "They stole this canyon from my grandfather."

"There are thieves everywhere."

She nodded. "Right here too."

"Closer than you think." Arnulfo nodded toward the camp. Sprigs of dust lifted into the air as a pair of distant trucks bounced and pounded across the open grass, heading for the corrals.

Wyatt moved closer behind Faye. "The security team…"

"We gotta go," Faye said. "Tell them we showed you a pistol, made you cooperate…"

"I could not stop you."

"You sure you'll be OK? You could come with us…"

"No, I will be fine. You had a gun. What could I do?" he shrugged.

Faye nodded her thanks. She handed Lynch's drone to Wyatt.

"Maybe you could drive out to meet them?" Wyatt said. "Talk to them. Slow them down a bit…"

"Si."

"And radio the sheriff."

"I hear he is already on his way."

"Good." Wyatt looked hard at Arnulfo. "They murdered a man. An artist, blond hair, up there," he pointed behind him. "On top of the cliff, near the petroglyphs."

Arnulfo's eyes widened.

"Must have buried him somewhere in this canyon. We have to go, but we'll contact the sheriff as soon as we can." Wyatt turned and moved closer to the corrals.

"Si." Arnulfo glanced around, then shouted toward Faye: "Take care of your horses."

"Always."

Arnulfo climbed into the truck, started the engine, and began driving toward the security team.

Faye dipped her body though the slatted fencing and went to the tack shed. She returned with one saddle and reigns, then went gently among the horses, mumbling softly to them. She brought a bay mare to the gate, where Wyatt stood, and slipped the bit into the horse's mouth. She handed the reigns to Wyatt. She saddled the mare and went back among the others. In a few minutes, she led a speckled gelding to the fence and saddled it as well. They led the horses through the gate and closed it behind them.

"I've been trying to get my balance back on a horse," Wyatt said.

"Your horse sense? No worries. It'll come back to you." She rose into her saddle and waited.

Wyatt handed the drone back to her, then put his foot in the stirrup and slid awkwardly across the saddle and into place. His mare stomped and shifted and he grabbed the saddle horn for balance.

"We'll try to keep a steady pace." She tightened her grip on the drone case.

"How far is it to your ranch?"

"The ranch boundary line is only about three miles from here, but the house is nearly twenty."

"Twenty?"

Wyatt could see the three pickups stopped, bunched together in the meadow, about a mile south.

"Don't worry, we'll get there by nightfall." She clicked her tongue and her horse began a quick trot. Wyatt's mare followed with a jolt. He tried to mimic Faye as she rose and fell with the horse's stride. His ass was going to be sore tonight.

Chapter 66

Relic had detached the chain from the four-wheeler and ridden it to the corrals. He could see Wyatt and Faye in the distance, trotting their horses toward the river. Two pickup trucks trailed them by about a half-mile, but his friends would soon lose them in the rough ground near the arroyo and the northern cliffs above the river. He turned off the engine and watched the corralled horses for a while, choosing which to ride, thinking about Old Man Snow, and Faye, and Wyatt.

He pulled the gate back and propped it open. He pulled a bunch of grass from the earth and offered it to a black mare. He stroked her nose and neck, speaking gently, letting her know he was a friend. He wrapped a bundle of her mane in his left hand and jumped across her back. She shied away, but he kept his balance and sat up across her shoulders. Clicking, he guided her to the back of the corral and herded the other horses through the gate.

He stopped and looked back toward the clearing on top of the ridge, the petroglyph that Winford and Lynch and Schmidt had killed to make their own. The dying man's voice filled his head again. "Hoax," the artist had said, and "treasure." He'd just done the rest – a dozen beautiful replicas. Relic thought of the panel of artwork, and the single petroglyph on that ridge, among all the phonies, that was real. Now, that treasure was hidden, in plain sight, just one of a dozen fakes the blond man had so skillfully chiseled into stone. No longer a lone treasure for anyone to find and exploit. Now, all of it a hoax no one would care to see.

Relic watched two pickups bounce across the terrain heading west, still following well behind Wyatt and Faye. They could not catch them now.

If Relic kept a steady pace, he could get to the dry creek bed, and the rocky ground beyond, before the men could turn and chase him. No one could follow him from there.

Relic rode the mare back and forth behind the other horses, yelling and whistling until they all began to move away together, toward the arroyo. He re-wrapped his left hand in her long, dark mane, jabbed his heels behind her stomach, and whooped at the top of his lungs until they all began to run, loose and easy, toward freedom.

Author's Note:

The idea that early Puebloan people may have etched petroglyphs of dinosaurs is the subject of some speculation. There seems little doubt that they found and understood dinosaur footprints – replicas of the tracks have appeared on traditional clothing. And the tracks are open and obvious enough, found along the Colorado River near panels of rock art above Moab, for example. Early people of the Southwest seem to have been aware of the unusual bones exposed in the open rock, like those now enshrined in Dinosaur National Park. But whether there are petroglyphs of the long-necked herbivores or sharp-toothed raptors is another question. Some say they see them among the more amorphous rock art, some say they exist only in our imaginations. A dramatic example of dinosaur petroglyphs, such as the ones envisioned in Raptor Canyon, would likely create a stir among archeologists and the public alike. If they do exist, may they forever be protected.

Acknowledgements:

I want to acknowledge my parents, family, colleagues, and accomplices. Thanks to all who understand their kinship with the planet and those who work in the service of their ideals. And I want to thank Ron for that hike to the top of Square Top Mountain in the Wind River Range, near the headwaters of the Green River, and Adam, Jeff, and Bridger for that stair-master climb to the Doll House above Spanish Bottom, near the confluence of the Green and Colorado Rivers; and I especially thank Doug and Dave for all the adventures and misadventures, hiking, canoeing, fishing, swimming. I am even grateful for the sore muscles, swamped canoes, and sudden whitewater swims. Everyone should spend all the time they need in the church of the great outdoors. May it never be organized by man nor entirely safe.

Thanks to my incredible wife Gina and my wonderful family for letting me disappear for hours and days at a time while working on this story and for their valued comments and contributions. I could not have written it without them. Special appreciation goes to Sarah, Ben, Adam, Sarajean, Nate, Anna, Ze, Natalie, Caitlin, and Azelea, and to Julie and Dave, just for being the wonderful people they are.

As always, thanks to Mom and Dad for all their patience and support over the years. Dad, the first copy of Raptor Canyon is for you.

I also want to thank Jim Dempsey, editor at Novel Gazing, for his encouragement, careful attention to detail, and insightful suggestions. I could not have finished this without him. And I thank Nate for his incredible cover art and book design and for his invaluable help with the technical aspects of the work.

Learn more about the author and his work at
awbaldwin.com

Buy now from a bookstore near you or amazon.com.

Also available from A.W. Baldwin:

Ethan's world turns upside-down when he slips off the
edge of red-rock cliffs into a world of twisting canyons,
ruthless looters, and midnight murders. Saved by a
moonshining hermit, Ethan must join a whitewater
rafting group and make his way back to civilization. But
someone in the canyons is killing to protect their illegal
dig for ancient treasures. Ethan must learn who he can
and cannot trust, survive the harsh desert, and unravel
the mysterious murders. The fight of his life begins
now...